MW01125924

GEMINI RISING

Mischievous Malamute Mystery Series Book 1

HARLEY CHRISTENSEN

Copyright © 2014 Harley Christensen

Cover Photos:
Copyright adimas — Illustration of DNA| Fotolia
Copyright yappingdog — Image of alley | yappingdog

All rights reserved. No part of this publication may be reproduced, distributed, or
transmitted in any form or by any means, including photocopying, recording, or
other electronic or mechanical methods, without the prior written permission of
the publisher, except in the case of brief quotations embodied in critical reviews
and certain other noncommercial uses permitted by copyright law.

ISBN-10: 1480195332
ISBN-13: 978-1480195332

*For Mark, Oskyr and Naoisha—my own mischievous motley crew
—you make me want to do the Snoopy Dance each and every day.*

To Carol, your copy of Who Moved My Cheese? *inspired me to
find out what I would do if I weren't afraid.*

*To my parents, for your love and support, and for believing I
could do anything I set my mind to.*

*In memory of Jazmine, Behr and Lacey—may your days be filled
with endless tails to chase.*

PROLOGUE

Life is funny sometimes.

You go through it believing you are a plain old Joe, or Jane, living a normal, mundane existence.

You work.

You pay bills.

You walk your dog.

You eat.

You sleep.

The point being, you get up every day and do it all over again, because nothing out of the ordinary ever really happens.

Right?

Here's the kicker: Once in a while Life throws in a bit of mischief—kind of like the snarky little brother you wish you could permanently lock in his room, rather than those few cherished times you've gotten away with when Mom wasn't looking —only much, much worse. And because you're expecting the same old same old, you're flabbergasted when Life punches you in the gut.

As you crumble to the ground, gasping for air, you might have that notorious *ah-ha* moment. You know the one I mean. The one where you come to the realization the experience was your wake-up call—a reminder you're alive and in control of your destiny—and to make the most of it.

The cynic in me thinks it's Life's not-so-funny way of reminding you who's really in control—the punch line being—you only *think* you are.

CHAPTER ONE

Shortly after 4 a.m. on Tuesday, I woke to a start, realizing it was garbage day and I'd forgotten to set mine out. Again. It was late November and though it doesn't get that cold in this part of the Southwest—certainly not like other parts of the country—the Saltillo tile was chilly on my feet as I jumped out of bed. Nicoh, my ninety-eight pound Alaskan Malamute—still on top of the bed and ever the helpful one—peered at me from under the blankets and pillows he managed to steal during the night, before returning to whatever doggie dreams he'd been having.

Ugh. Someday I'd get my bed back. Today wasn't going to be that day. The city's garbage collection truck would arrive in ten minutes, so I grabbed the trash bag from the kitchen and opened the door. It was still dark outside but the moon hung lazily in the sky, providing a single source of light as I moved through the backyard and out the iron gate that led to the alley where I shared a dumpster with my neighbors.

Except for the occasional hum of a passing car on the nearby street, it was silent. With my free hand, I wiped the sleep from my eyes and cursed myself again before tossing the lid of the dumpster, which as usual, was sticky and nasty. Just wonderful. I firmly grabbed the trash bag with both hands to toss it in but stopped short when I noticed the smudgy reddish-brown imprint my hand left against the starkness of the white bag. I started to look more closely when a putrid metallic stench filled the air, forcing me to focus my attention on the open dumpster.

I swallowed hard and tried not to breathe in too deeply as I looked over the edge, expecting to find a package of rotten meat or at most, a dead animal. I gasped in disbelief and shock at the horrific scene before me.

A girl's thin frame, clad only in a hot pink tank top and jeans, nestled among the trash bags and lawn trimmings. Her bare arms —flung above her head as if celebrating a touchdown—were a sharp contrast to her legs, which were bent in awkward, unnatural angles beneath her.

Disturbing as her body was, her face told an even more vicious and sinister tale. No, there was no celebration. Someone had made sure of that when they erased whatever smile she'd had —the wrinkle her nose made as she laughed, the twinkle that glistened in her eyes—replacing it with a death mask of pulverized flesh and bone, rendering her faceless. Unrecognizable. Blood congealed in her hair, likely once long and lush, now matted and tangled into oblivion.

Though sickened at the sight, an immense sadness came over me—who could be so cruel, so hateful—to end her life so violently? I clenched my fists as sadness turned to anger.

The blaring horn of the garbage truck disrupted my thoughts. I dropped the forgotten trash bag as I swirled to face it and waved my arms frantically at the driver, who looked at me through his hazy window with disgust. I was clearly messing with his schedule. I ignored the profanities he barked in my direction and continued to flap my arms, begging him to stop.

"Sir, please call 911!" I yelled. "There's a body in the dumpster!"

The worker pulled the brake on his truck, jumped out and joined me at the dumpster, probably doubting my sanity. After a whiff and an unexpected eyeful, he turned away and vomited loudly against my neighbor's retaining wall. Several seconds later he coughed, pulled out his cell phone and called 911.

Finally, he addressed me, "Hon, you seriously could've warned me."

I shook my head and for once, held my tongue.

CHAPTER TWO

Detective Jonah Ramirez stepped out of the cruiser and checked his watch. 4:45 a.m. Man, did it ever get it any easier? he wondered to himself. After sixteen years on the job—eleven of them in Homicide—he knew the answer. Over time, he tried to put the names and faces behind him, letting them blend into one another until they became less and less distinct. Still, the memories haunted him. Drove him. He shrugged as he surveyed the scene unfolding in the alley.

The crime scene unit had been dispatched shortly after the 911 call at 4:07 a.m., so Robert Jabawski and his team were in the midst of their investigation.

"Whatcha got for me, Jabba?" Ramirez asked as he reached the lead technician, calling the man by his nickname.

The stout tech grimaced as he came up from bent knees—an old football injury, he always claimed—pushing thick black-framed glasses to the top of his head before squinting at Ramirez.

"Nice of you to finally show up, Detective," he quipped. "You bring me any coffee or are you just here to block my light?"

Ramirez chuckled, then handed his old friend the usual offering: a venti-sized Starbucks Pike Place Roast with six Splenda packets and a splash of half-and-half. Jabawski sniffed the contents and nodded in approval.

"We've got ourselves a female victim—no identification— with extensive trauma to the face and head. Damage was inflicted elsewhere, but her body made its way into the dumpster before she expired."

"A beating?" Ramirez questioned.

Jabawski nodded. "Yeah, it's looking that way. There was a significant amount of rage driving this perp. Girl's got no face left. Here, see for yourself." The tech moved a few feet to where two members of his team were working.

Death filled his nostrils as Ramirez followed Jabawski to the dumpster. Though he'd grown accustomed to her pungent fragrance over the years, it was Death's indiscriminate vicious- ness that set him on edge. As the techs continued to work, he leaned in to observe her current reaping. Jabawski had been right, Death had been brutal—savage even—as she snatched the girl's life into her rakish clutches. Triumphant, no doubt, as she claimed her victory, despite the means with which she obtained it. He knew it was her way. Death—like Life—didn't play fair. Ramirez shook his head in frustration and turned his attention back to Jabawski.

"Anything to work with yet?" he asked.

"We're still collecting, but it's not promising," Jabawski replied somberly. "We're working with a dumpster and an alley, not exactly a CSU's dream."

"Witnesses?" Ramirez prompted.

"Nope. The owner of the house directly behind us found the victim while taking her trash out. Her name is Arianna Jackson. City's trash guy arrived within a minute or two after that. She waved him down and got him to call 911. Anyway, he's over by his truck. Despite having chucked his morning McMuffin all over the wall, he has quite a mouth on him. Ms. Jackson is with your guys in her backyard." Jabawski thumbed over his left shoulder.

As Ramirez started in that direction, Jabawski called after him, laughing, "Watch out for the big bad wolf, he's got a mouth on him, too."

* * *

Everything was moving in slow motion. Or at least it appeared to be. Police officers and crime scene technicians swarmed like worker bees from the hive, scouting out their surroundings meticulously, in hope of finding even the most minuscule of clues.

I'd spoken to several officers and carefully detailed my actions before finding the body. One officer eventually allowed me to retrieve Nicoh, who had awoken from his doggie slumber and—not one to be left out—had gone into full howl mode. Not pretty given the hour.

Unfortunately, it also hadn't done much to detract the small crowd of onlookers congregating at the alley's entrance. Now that I was safely in his sights, his piercing howls subsided, though there were still the occasional whoo-whoos as techs and officers passed. If anybody was going to get the last word, it would be Nicoh.

While we waited, I offered the crime scene techs shoe prints, fingerprints and paw prints for exclusionary purposes, along with a couple other items I thought might be useful, including a list of neighbors.

At first, they indulged me, but after a short while, most resorted to a tight smile, a nod of the head or a pat on the back before politely asking me to return to my backyard to wait for Detective Ramirez, the lead investigator on the case, to arrive.

With nothing left to do, I resorted to flicking paint chips off the weathered bench where I sat. Nicoh grumbled in disgust—

hopefully at the situation and not my choice of tasks—before sighing and placing his large head on his paws.

We carried on like this for a bit until a dark figure strode purposefully through the back gate. I had to keep from gasping audibly as I took in the tall, imposing stranger. Wavy black hair framed tanned skin, a strong, chiseled jaw and piercing green eyes. Though dressed in faded jeans, worn cowboy boots and a semi-pressed button-down shirt, his demeanor indicated he was the man in charge. His expression gave nothing away but I knew he was sizing us up, analyzing us in his cop-like way.

"Alaskan Malamute?" he asked.

"Very good, Detective Ramirez. Most people assume he's a Siberian Husky or wolf-hybrid, but Nicoh's 100 percent Malamute," I replied. "All ninety-eight pounds of him."

Nicoh sat up straighter and whoo-whoo'd with delight because of course, any conversation he was the subject of had to be a good one, right? Some protector, I mused.

"You know who I am." It was more of a statement than a question, though Ramirez arched an eyebrow in mock surprise.

"Well, I've been interviewed by most everyone here, excluding the media, of course," I subconsciously snarled out the word "media," which ignited a flicker of amusement in Ramirez's eyes. "Anyway, several of the officers mentioned you were the lead detective, noted I would need to speak with you and told me that my animal and I would need to sit quietly and wait until you arrived on the scene," I paraphrased the actual conversations, but was sure Ramirez caught the sarcasm. "So, now that you are here, how can I help you, Detective?"

* * *

Ramirez hadn't been sure what to make of Jabawski's last

comment, but as he entered the gate leading into Arianna Jackson's backyard, two things struck him.

First was the large canine. Surrounded by a dark mask, its eyes reflected off the lights, giving them an eerie, copper cast. It bore a strong, muscular body with a bushy, curly tail, draped carelessly along its back as it rose to acknowledge his arrival. Its pointed, megaphone-like ears jutted forward. If not mistaken, it was an Alaskan Malamute—not a breed he'd often seen in a city like Phoenix.

The second thing he noticed was the woman the dog pressed himself against protectively. She wore an oversized crimson Henley, black running pants and ASICS with fluorescent yellow shoelaces. Her long dark hair was pulled into a high ponytail on the back of her head. Angled bangs shaded her eyes, though Ramirez could tell they were bright blue, with a fleck of something he couldn't quite make out, given the distance between them. Whatever it was, it was striking. She wore no makeup but had a healthy flush to her cheeks. While tall and slender, her composed manner indicated she could handle both herself and that big dog, if needed.

She wasn't rude but seemed eager to proceed, so he dispensed with the small talk and got down to business. As he questioned her, he found her direct and to the point, with a great deal of confidence and control. Her eyes met his with each response, her voice never wavering as she detailed her steps. A cool customer for someone who had stumbled upon a body in her dumpster, he noted. It didn't mean she was immune to it, just that she'd tucked it away until prepared to deal with it. He'd seen it before—she didn't want to lose control in front of him. She was a tough one, for sure.

After they finished their discussion, he offered to call someone to come and stay with her or to take her elsewhere. As he'd expected, she politely thanked him for his offer but declined.

He gave her his card, told her he'd be in touch and scratched Nicoh behind the ears as he turned to leave.

Violet, like a brewing storm, he decided—that was the color of the flecks in her eyes.

* * *

Detective Ramirez quickly put me at ease as he questioned me and for the first time in a long while, I found another person's company strangely comforting. In fact, I didn't relish the thought of him leaving, but holding him hostage with my feminine wiles wasn't an option, considering the circumstances.

I kicked myself. Seriously? Thoughts like that were so unlike me, I must have been suffering from exhaustion. I sighed to myself and let Ramirez go before I made a complete idiot out of myself. Well, almost.

"One last question?" I asked.

Ramirez looked at me intently. "Shoot."

"You got a first name, Detective?" Eck, I mentally winced at my obviousness.

Ramirez broke into a small smile. "Jonah. Good night, Ms. Jackson."

"AJ," I countered.

"Good night, AJ." And with that, he strode out of the gate, just as easily as he'd come in.

Nicoh peered at me—a glint of mischief in his eyes—and for a moment, I thought he was going to follow. I know how you feel, buddy, I thought. I know how you feel.

CHAPTER THREE

He stood on the fringe of the crowd, smirking to himself as he eavesdropped on their whispered speculations about what had transpired in the alley. If they only knew.

Fools.

The task had been completed. Not to his satisfaction, of course, but completed. One more detail lingered. After years of waiting, it would soon be finished.

For now, he needed to focus on the end goal—obtain the final piece of the puzzle and destroy anyone who got in his way.

CHAPTER FOUR

Getting back to normal—uh yeah, good luck with that. After finding the body, I tried my best, but something was off. Several days later, as Nicoh and I walked to the park, I reflected on what bothered me. True, the incident had been a shocker. It wasn't as though I'd seen many dead bodies before, certainly not ones mutilated so barbarically. I shuddered, the image forever tattooed in my memory.

As unpleasant as it had been, that wasn't it. It was almost as though I'd missed something, something I'd seen and not registered. I kicked myself, my eyes had been trained better than that. As a freelance photographer, I was familiar with visualizing subject matter from multiple angles and perspectives. Yet this time, it eluded me. Maybe it was something I hadn't seen? A feeling, perhaps?

I continued to rehash the events of that morning and was so engrossed I nearly ran Nicoh head-on into the Greyhound trio—Molly, Maxine and Maybelline. Fortunately, I adjusted my step just in time and nodded to their owner—a man whose name I'll admit I don't remember. He nodded in return while the dogs did their usual sniff-and-wag bit.

Nicoh straightened his stance more than usual—head and ears held high, chest thrust forward—perhaps to compensate for my clumsiness, but certainly not for the affections of the elegant trio. Nope, he had his eye on a she-devil named Pandora, a silver and white Keeshond that lived around the corner with a retired lawyer. Sadly, I didn't remember his name either, but Pandora managed to find her way into our yard to visit on occasion, so her lawyer and I knew each other by dog and yard. Our little neighborhood was funny that way.

Situated in east Phoenix on the borders of Scottsdale and Paradise Valley, we were nestled into an area that was older than most, but where the homes and yards were well-maintained, despite their age. Citrus trees and date palms lined the streets, providing a canopy from the blistering Arizona sun without blocking the view of the surrounding mountains. A once highly-coveted neighborhood among the up-and-coming and affluent, the attraction of newer, cookie-cutter neighborhoods farther north had lured residents away over the past ten to fifteen years. While lacking personality, these newer neighborhoods provided many conveniences—high-end outdoor malls, restaurants, theaters, etc. —within a stone's throw in every direction, converting the congested neighborhoods into mini cities, which appealed to the masses.

A few diehards, like my parents, stayed on in the old neighborhood, meticulously caring for and upgrading their lovely Ranch-style home with its sprawling yard and manicured gardens until they died unexpectedly two years ago. The house had been left to me—their only child. I could not afford such a house on my freelance earnings alone, but my parents had paid cash for it and then set aside a monthly stipend for maintenance and updates, which was also willed to me. I couldn't bear to part with it yet. It was the house they loved so much, where I'd grown-up and created many incredible memories. The memories and the house were all I had left of my parents. A lump grew in my throat as I thought of them. Missed them.

I was jerked to the present by my companion's annoyed whoo-whoos. We had reached the park. No distractions while on his time, Nicoh reminded me. *Doggie translation:* Time to get down to business.

CHAPTER FIVE

Ramirez felt uneasy as he approached the house. He had initially liked the spunky gal. Maybe a bit too much. True, she had been annoyingly abrupt at their first meeting, but he'd also found her direct and brutally honest—traits he admired. Absently, he shook his head. Even though experience and an ever-increasing mound of concrete evidence told him what he was about to do was just, the task gave him no pleasure. He exhaled deeply as he knocked on the front door.

* * *

Nicoh and I had returned from our nightly jaunt around the neighborhood when there was a knock on the door. Strange that the person wouldn't ring the doorbell, I thought. Nicoh simply huffed at the interruption. It was dinnertime, after all. Some guard dog, I grumbled. So glad someone had his priorities straight. My thoughts on Nicoh's questionable qualities ceased as I opened the door to a grim-faced detective.

"Oh, good evening, Detective Ramirez." I surprised myself by managing to sound half way put-together, though inside I felt anything but.

"Good evening, Ms. Jackson," the Homicide detective replied evenly, though I noticed he was shifting uneasily from one foot to the other. Uh-oh, I thought. This can't be good.

"Please, call me AJ," I reminded him. "I assume you are here about the case? Do you have more questions for me? Have there been any new developments? Has the poor girl been identified? Has her family been notified? Are there any leads?" Ok, I'll admit it, perhaps babbling nonstop and getting to the point should be mutually exclusive.

* * *

Ramirez suppressed a smile when AJ fired-off a series of questions the moment he'd said hello. She had been much the same way the morning she'd found the girl in the dumpster. A casual observer would have thought her a calm, cool and collected customer, undaunted by the tragic circumstances that surrounded her. He had the benefit of training and experience, however, and knew the type well. It was a front, a shell she created to keep everything and everyone at an arm's length when the world around her was out of control. By presenting the tough exterior, she was able to retain some semblance of that control, even if it was only of herself and her emotions.

She had proven his point when she declined his offer to call a friend or family member to join her that morning. Even before he'd asked, he'd known she would turn him down. In fact, she seemed to have anticipated the offer when she quickly but graciously declined, as though purposely willing him to move on, to focus his attention elsewhere. Anywhere, but on her.

He forced his thoughts back to the present and to the matter at hand. Given her nature, she would expect directness, he decided.

"Actually, yes, there have been developments, AJ," he began. "We have identified the victim but not notified the next-of-kin because there are none. We have no suspects—a few persons-of-interest, at most and at this point, only theories on the motive," he paused, but she looked at him expectantly, so he pressed on. "The victim has been identified as Victoria Winestone, a commercial real estate agent from Los Angeles. Does the name sound familiar to you?"

"No, I don't believe so," she responded firmly, though he could feel a cloud of unease surround her. "Should it?"

He ignored her question and continued, "I'd like to show you a couple of pictures. One is a copy of Ms. Winestone's California driver's license, taken a few years ago, and the other is from her LinkedIn profile, which is more recent."

Ramirez removed the pictures from the worn file folder he'd been holding. He placed each photo in front of her, studying her as she peered with interest, first at one, then the other. After a few moments, her expression transformed from one of curiosity to another of surprise and confusion, her mouth forming a tiny "o."

"As you can see, AJ, the resemblance is quite remarkable." Though she didn't reply, he moved on. "We compared Ms. Winestone's fingerprints to the ones you had on file from your free-lance work with the County. Again, the similarities were remarkable. Finally, we compared Ms. Winestone's DNA to the sample you graciously provided at the crime scene," Ramirez paused to catch his breath, collect his thoughts and make sure AJ was still with him. She was, though her expression hadn't changed.

He delivered the rest, the part he had been dreading since his arrival, "The thing is, AJ, the DNA samples matched. In fact, they were *exact* matches." Ramirez placed a hand firmly on her arm. "Having said that, I have to ask you again. Are you sure you have

never met this woman—murdered feet away from your home—
who, by all accounts, was your identical twin sister?"

* * *

I gasped at his words, my mind reeling as I attempted to register
their meaning. Though her hair was several shades lighter—a
honey blonde compared to my reddish-brown—the girl in the
pictures did bear a striking resemblance. Her eyes were the same
crystal blue, speckled with a hint of violet. A quirk of a smile
played on the left-hand side of her mouth, turning it up ever so
slightly, as though amused by something only she was aware of.
Perhaps an inside joke meant solely for her? I, too, had that quirk.

I scoffed. What Detective Ramirez was suggesting was
beyond ridiculous. A twin? An identical twin, at that? It wasn't
even possible. I was an only child. If my parents had still been
alive, they would have found the conversation laughable.

Still, the fact remained. A girl had been murdered. Brutally.
Her face bashed in, her body broken and disposed of like trash in
my alley. How could this have happened? And why?

Suddenly, the ground felt as though it was shifting as nausea
set in and bile threatened the base of my throat. Oh, no—I was
not going to faint. Or hurl. Or cry. Or burst into some other crazy
display of emotions. I squeezed my hands into fists and clutched
them at my side, waiting for the feelings to subside. I knew I was
being silly. Reactions like this were normal and probably
expected, especially given the circumstances. They just weren't
my normal.

Yet somehow, I knew from that moment on, normal was going
to be a thing of the past.

Nicoh grumbled quietly, as if in agreement.

CHAPTER SIX

After that revelation, "no" was all I could manage, as a significant amount of brain-freeze had developed.

"There's more," Ramirez said. This time he would not meet my gaze.

"What?" I squeaked.

"Two years ago, your parents, Richard and Eileen Jackson perished when their plane crashed while in transit from Albuquerque to Colorado Springs."

I shuddered at the memory but added, "Yes, along with their pilot, Phil Stevens."

"According to the official report," Ramirez nodded toward the thickly-bound document he was holding, "all three passengers were accounted for and identified by their dental records. The investigator ruled the cause of the crash as engine failure, which was consistent with the pilot's final communication. In the end, it was considered an untimely, albeit tragic accident and the investigation was subsequently closed." This was not news to me, so I simply nodded in agreement.

"A couple of days ago, I was in Starbucks getting my morning

brew when I was approached by two men who introduced themselves as private investigators from Los Angeles. Although I was
skeptical, they indicated they had some information to offer. Typically with PIs, it's the other way around, so I decided to hear
them out.

"They were searching for a client of theirs who had recently
gone missing after heading to Phoenix. That client was Victoria
Winestone. Unfortunately, I had to break the news about
her death.

"As it turned out, Victoria had hired them six months earlier
to quietly look into your parent's accident—everything from the
events leading up to the crash to the investigation that followed."
Ramirez stopped briefly to let this sink in.

Frankly, I was dumbfounded. "Why would this girl go to the
trouble of hiring PIs to investigate an accidental plane crash?
More importantly, why was she even interested in my family in
the first place?"

"According to the PIs, Victoria was convinced the crash was
not accidental. She felt bigger forces were at play. Forces that not
only affected your family but hers as well. The thing is, Victoria's
parents recently died, too," he said solemnly.

"Wow, that is awful, though I still don't see the correlation…"

When I didn't finish my thought, Ramirez completed it for
me, "I know it's not going to make any sense, but there was a
correlation, a connection between all of you. Victoria had proof of
it. Proof you were her sister. Proof you were both adopted." He
paused to look at me and for a moment, I wondered what he saw:
fear, disbelief, horror?

Whatever it was, he let pass and continued on, though his
voice had grown quiet, "The PIs indicated Victoria had known
about you and the adoption for some time but weren't sure why
she hadn't made contact. They were surprised when she suddenly

left them a voicemail, indicating her plans to travel to Arizona, for you. It was the last time they heard from her. The next day, she was dead."

CHAPTER SEVEN

My head was spinning. Had I fallen asleep or been knocked unconscious, left to fend for myself in some sort of bizarro alternate reality? Or, better yet, perhaps I was being punk'd? I was sure Ramirez thought I had lost my marbles as I swiveled my head from side to side, searching for the hidden cameras. Finding none, I took a deep breath and opted to stare at the worn tread on my tennis shoes while I mulled things over.

"Are you ok, AJ?" Ramirez asked, concern filling his voice.

After a moment, I looked up at him and nodded absently. "In the last twenty minutes, I've found out"—I held my fingers up as I counted—"that *one*: the girl brutally murdered a few hundred feet away from where we are standing was not only my sister but my dead twin sister; *two*: I was adopted, and *three*: according to this dead twin sister, my parent's deaths were not the result of an unfortunate cosmic accident, but of some evil force out there killing adoptive parents." I laughed, perhaps a bit too harshly. "Seriously? This has all the makings of a bad Lifetime movie. Now that you've shared, what is it you expect me to do with all this information, Detective?"

Ramirez nodded in understanding. He had entered her world,

basically dumped all over it and then offered nothing in return but confusion and drama. She had every right to question him. He owed her. It was time to come clean.

"Shortly after Victoria's body was identified, the local FBI swooped in, debriefed us, rounded up all pertinent files and told us they would take it from there. So officially, we're off the case." I started to say something, but he held up his hand. "To make matters worse, every single time those guys take over one of our cases, it conveniently gets filed into their black hole of bureaucracy. In the meantime, any leads there might have been will go cold.

Unfortunately, this also means Victoria Winestone will end up a statistic—another nameless victim whose justice will never come—and that does not sit right with me. Not one bit." Ramirez became quiet for a moment, his eyes haunted, before turning to face me.

"I took a huge risk coming here and telling you all of this, but I had a gut feeling about you—one that told me you would want to know more and the opportunity to do more."

I shook my head in disbelief and nearly laughed at the absurdity of that comment.

"What is it you think I can do, Detective? I am nobody. A photographer with a dog who has bad manners and even worse breath. None of that qualifies me for the starring role as Nancy Drew."

Ramirez chuckled. "Dog-related behavioral and hygiene issues aside, you've got a lot more going for you than you think. Plus, you've got two PIs at your disposal."

At my furrowed brow, he quickly added, "Don't worry. They don't have your name yet—and I won't pass it along until you agree—but they're more than ready to get back to work on this. I'll admit, while they aren't saints, they are decent, hard-working guys—guys who don't like it when their client gets herself killed on their watch. They want to make this right, AJ, and I fully believe you can trust them to do it."

"But what if your bosses or the FBI find out? Surely they'll realize the information about Victoria's identity was leaked from somewhere?"

"I will deal with it as it comes."

He provided me with the PIs particulars, scratching Nicoh behind the ears before turning to leave. As he pulled the door behind him, he looked at me, his gaze intense.

"AJ?"

"Yeah?"

"Watch your back. My gut also tells me this is far from over."

"Is your gut ever wrong, Detective?"

"Good or bad, there's a first time for everything."

CHAPTER EIGHT

My brain was still swimming from Ramirez's visit when the front door opened and my best friend, Leah Campbell, popped her head in. Despite the concern crinkling at the corners of her eyes and mouth, I smiled at the sight of her. Tired of the Sunshine Barbie nickname her co-workers at the newspaper had bestowed upon her, Leah recently rebelled by lopping off her long shimmering locks in favor of a shorter, spiky cut—which still made her adorable, but gave her more of an edgy, precocious appearance. Think Meg Ryan in *Addicted to Love*.

She offered me one of the iced lattes she was holding, then slipped a doggie treat from her pocket and tossed it into the air. Nicoh inhaled it without chewing, all while giving her one of his famous I-almost-had-to-wait looks. I took a long sip of my beverage before nodding in satisfaction and then proceeded to fill her in on my conversation with Ramirez. She said nothing until I finished, though her usually perky features were grim as she listened intently.

"You ok?" she asked after a long moment, self-consciously attempting to tuck a stray spike behind her ear, only to have it errantly jut in the opposite direction. "It's a lot to digest for anyone, Ajax. Even you."

She used the nickname she had given me years earlier. Not that I liked being compared to cleaning products but she had a point—despite my sometimes outwardly abrasive and direct nature, I always managed to get the job done.

I shrugged. I certainly didn't feel like I was living up to my nickname today. I turned to the kitchen counter, where I had spread out the notes for my next photo assignment—a failed attempt at distracting myself from the day's events.

"What's this?" Leah asked, eyeing me carefully. "I thought you were going to take a couple of days off?"

"I was, but wallowing in self-pity doesn't pay the bills or feed this gluttonous beast." I scratched Nicoh behind his massive, downy-soft ears and was rewarded with a low whoo-whoo of approval.

"Besides," I continued, "Charlie basically threatened me if I didn't get the shots of his new Tempe Town Lake condo done." I waved to the paperwork in front of me. "Apparently, he has a deadline for another hoity-toity magazine."

Ahh…Charlie Wilson. My client. Born with a titanium spoon in his mouth. The spoiled grandson of a software magnate. Never worked a day in his life, but notorious for throwing very public, Oscar award-winning—or at the very least, Daytime Emmy award-winning—tantrums. And, to keep up appearances, the tantrums surfaced daily—sometimes even hourly—though thankfully, I hadn't had the displeasure of being on the receiving end. Yet. I wasn't inclined to make this the first time, either.

I should have been grateful Charlie had chosen me as his photographer. Of course, he had only done so because he felt we had history, if you could call attending the same high school history.

Our working relationship started at a party we both attended after returning from college—me from UCLA and Charlie from Harvard. While rekindling said history, Charlie generously offered to throw some work my way.

Charlie turned out to be more demanding and difficult than all my other clients combined, but his jobs not only paid the bulk of my bills, they provided me with the word-of-mouth needed to get my business off the ground.

At the time, I was appreciative, as I had recently started my freelance photography business, aptly named Mischievous Malamute after a few photoshoot mishaps featuring my canine companion. Thankfully, it had never been more than a couple misplaced dinner rolls or uprooted props, but it was still embarrassing. In the end, naming the business after my companion seemed appropriate—not only as a warning to future clients but a reminder to myself to keep him in check while on location.

I sighed and returned my attention to Leah, who was still focused intently on me. She knew, just as I did, Charlie's project provided a temporary distraction. I'd have to deal with Ramirez's news sooner or later. Knowing me as she did, she decided sooner was better and jumped in head-first.

"What do you want to do, Ajax? And, more importantly, what can I do to help?"

CHAPTER NINE

After much debate, Leah and I agreed—actually, Leah decided and I agreed—it couldn't hurt to meet the private investigators to get their take on the situation.

Using the business card Ramirez left, I made an appointment with Stanton Investigations of L.A. The administrative assistant, Anna Goodwin, told me Abe and Elijah Stanton were still in Phoenix awaiting my call and would meet me at Starbucks the next morning. I'd never dealt with PIs before, so Leah offered to be my backup in case things "got rough." Her words, not mine. I agreed though I got the distinct impression she was hoping a pair of Thomas Magnums would show up in a red Ferrari.

Leah, Nicoh—my backup-backup—and I arrived at Starbucks the following morning fifteen minutes early. Nicoh and I selected a corner seat on the covered outdoor patio while Leah grabbed beverages and snacks. I scoped the area but didn't see any PI-types lurking, so I settled for nervously picking the corners of my notepad. I doubted I would be able to calm down enough to take any notes, but as a reporter, Leah felt it was crucial to carry props. Of course, I'd forced her to leave the tape recorder at home, so she settled for a small notepad like mine.

We also decided against divulging her occupation. I needed to get information out of these guys, not send them running.

Leah came out a short time later, laden with caffeinated beverages and goodies. I grumbled I wasn't going to be able to eat, to which Leah smartly replied Nicoh would be more than happy to help me. Did I mention she'd already bought him his own maple scone? No wonder he was so incorrigible. And stocky. I was too nervous to chastise her, so I nibbled on the corner of my blueberry scone before Nicoh had the chance to claim it.

Minutes later, two ex-football player types entered the patio. Our PIs had arrived. Abe and Elijah Stanton were clearly brothers, both standing over 6 feet 3 inches, clad in black leather jackets, jeans and wayfarers, with the same angular features and sky-blue eyes. That was where the similarity ended.

Abe wore his tawny hair shorter with gelled spikes on the top —that whole Brad Pitt bedhead look guys claim they don't spend hours in front of the mirror perfecting—a black t-shirt and black Doc Marten boots.

While Elijah's hair fell to his shoulders in messy sun-bleached waves, the rest of him was anything but, with his immaculately-pressed button-down shirt that matched his eyes and expensive-looking loafers. Though I put them both in their early-to-mid thirties, it was up in the air as to which brother was the eldest. I looked over at Leah—who'd gone from an annoyingly tidy scone-eater to drooling mouth-breather—and kicked her as I rose from the table to greet them.

Fortunately, Leah collected herself as introductions were made and Nicoh gave them his sniff of approval. Though both stole glances at me when they thought I wasn't looking—likely due to my resemblance to Victoria—Elijah quickly started things off, indicating their intention to keep the meeting informal by outlining the information they'd gathered at Victoria's request and answering questions that surfaced as a result.

I was too antsy to tackle the tough stuff up front, so I asked them to give us a bit of background on themselves. I wasn't sure what I expected, but it wasn't their unabridged life history.

The Stanton brothers were born and raised in Salinas, California by a Highway Patrol officer and a high school history teacher. Like their father—a former college athlete—both excelled in football and were awarded full athletic scholarships, Abe first to the University of Southern California and Elijah two years later to my alma mater, UCLA. That cleared up my older vs. younger brother question.

Abe graduated with honors with a degree in Criminal Justice and immediately signed up for the Los Angeles Police Academy. After graduating from the academy six months later, he spent his requisite time on Metro patrol assignments, before competing for and being promoted to Police Detective.

Elijah, meanwhile, also graduated with honors with degrees in both Law and Business Administration but unlike his brother, struggled for direction for the first time in his life. Working as a clerk and research assistant in a top L.A. law firm had been interesting—and paid the bills—but didn't inspire the passion in him he dreamed it would. He wasn't afraid of hard work, and did enjoy the research, but couldn't see himself becoming a barrister for the next forty years.

Around the same time, Abe had begun to fester over the never-ending stream of bureaucratic red tape he encountered on a daily basis. No matter how tirelessly he worked, his efforts were routinely quashed for political reasons. After a particularly difficult period, he came to the overwhelming realization that unless he made a change, he would forever face the inability to make the type of difference he envisioned.

The brothers had each reached crossroads. Both wanted to affect change and be in control of how they went about it. Even if they only managed to do in small pieces over time, it was better than being at the mercy of people with ulterior motives, standing by going through the motions or worse yet, doing nothing. After much discussion, they combined the best of their skills—Elijah's knowledge of criminal justice and law enforcement and Abe's of law, business and research—and started a private investigation firm.

Starting small, they got leads from their former workplaces—including Elijah's law firm—and built their business on delivering thorough, consistent results in a professional, honest and timely manner.

The strong work ethic they'd learned from their parents, coupled with their tenacity and drive served them well. Within a short time, they had a steady flow of work—solely due to word of mouth—and their business thrived.

They splurged by opening a small office and hiring Anna, a former co-worker of Elijah's, to handle all scheduling and billing and more frequently, to assist with research. It was a win-win situation, Anna loved the autonomy the brothers gave her to run the operation and they were free to work out in the field.

Meanwhile, Dad and Mom—now retired—couldn't have been more proud of their sons. Of course, both expressed concern over their sons being more than 300 miles from home, though Abe and Elijah suspected both were making noise to cover their excitement. They would no longer need to make excuses for the additional trips to L.A.—their dad for his sporting events and mom for the surplus of shopping venues. We all laughed at the subterfuge.

I enjoyed Abe and Elijah's sharing of their background so much, I'd almost forgotten the purpose of the meeting. I said almost.

"So, how did you come to be here in Phoenix?" I asked.

"Way to be a buzz-kill, Ajax," Leah growled, loud enough for Abe and Elijah to hear.

Eyebrows lifted at my nickname, but Abe replied, "As Detective Ramirez mentioned, Victoria was our client. Two weeks ago, she left a voicemail indicating she was heading to Phoenix. It was the last time we heard from her. When she didn't respond to any of our phone calls or texts, we hopped in the car. After we arrived, we stopped at the police precinct down in Central Phoenix, introduced ourselves as PIs and showed them Victoria's picture.

"Ramirez must have been vigilant in circulating the details of the case—something about a bottle of thirty-year-old single malt —because no sooner had the words left our mouths, the desk sergeant supplied us with Ramirez's contact information, height, weight, shoe size, favorite flavor of ice cream…" We all chuckled in unison.

Elijah continued, "We were also able to find out Ramirez got his caffeine fix around the same time each morning," he glanced around, "at this Starbucks. So we took the opportunity to catch up with him.

"Of course, we still hadn't received confirmation Victoria was dead—the chatty Cathy desk sergeant hadn't managed to divulge that bit of information—though we already suspected something was up. I mean, if a Homicide detective is trading $1200 bottles of scotch for information, it can't be good.

"Anyway, Ramirez was suspicious at first, but once we gave him the condensed version of our background"—he paused to smile at me as I realized I had erroneously made the comment about their life history out loud—"and shared our connection to Victoria, he told us of her murder." Elijah looked away and Abe bowed his head, quietly studying his folded hands.

"I'm so sorry," I murmured, "she was more than a client—"

"She was a *client*," Abe snarked, taking me by surprise.

"I'm sorry. I didn't mean to imply…" I stammered, as Leah shot me a terse look that told me to shut up.

"No apologies necessary, AJ," Elijah said, his voice quiet. "What my brother means is Victoria was our client first. Working on a case like this, for as long as we have, you get to know some-one, especially when she puts as much in as she gets. It's hard not to care. So, yes, though we worked side by side as professionals, Victoria was more than our client. She'd become our friend."

"How did Victoria find you in the first place?" Leah asked, quickly shifting the subject.

"We'd taken on several projects for Platinum International, the real estate firm where she was employed, and though we never worked with her directly, she was familiar with our work," Elijah replied.

"Yeah, surprised the heck out of us." Abe smiled at the memory. "She was the first client who actually made an appoint-ment to meet us at our office. We hadn't physically been there in months—Anna keeps things running smoothly—so we raced there to make sure everything was still in order. Of course, Victoria arrived ahead of us, and she and Anna were chatting away like old friends, in our meticulously-organized and taste-fully-decorated office. And there sat Anna, with a coy, knowing smile."

"She knew what the two of you were up to," I commented with a light chuckle.

Abe, obviously no longer peeved at me, laughed. "She knew we'd come rushing to fix things, which meant we owed her a big fat raise for doubting her abilities."

"Lesson learned?" Leah teased.

They both laughed and nodded before Elijah turned the conversation back to their meeting with Ramirez.

"Anyway, Ramirez seemed like a good guy—and though he told us he'd been removed from the case earlier that morning—we thought perhaps he could help.

"Ramirez might have mentioned this, but when Victoria first hired us six months ago, it was to look into your parent's plane crash." I nodded, so he continued, "Victoria's story started before that, with the death of her parents, Joseph and Susan Winestone. You may have heard of them?"

We shook our heads. "No? Well, they made their fortune designing and building some of the most elite golf courses and resorts in the world—from California to Florida and Hawaii in the USA—to Australia, Scotland, Spain, etc."

"Oh my, yes! I remember them now," Leah exclaimed. "In fact, when they scouted locations in Arizona five years ago—" I kicked her hard before she inadvertently divulged she was a reporter. "Uh, I saw them being interviewed on the local news." I smiled at her sweetly, to which she pinched me under the table. I didn't dare look but was pretty sure she'd drawn blood.

If Abe or Elijah noticed our little squabble, they didn't let on. Abe continued where his brother had left off, "Anyway, the Winestones were taking the new Jag out for a spin along the Pacific Coast Highway. At one point during their trip, between Malibu and Santa Monica, the car veered, crashed through the divider and tumbled down the embankment, killing them both instantly."

"According to witnesses, the driver—Susan Winestone—never hit the brakes, nor appeared to be speeding. The crash investigators indicated the condition of that portion of the road had been good at the time of the accident—no potholes, dips, etc. —and the weather had been dry and clear. Technicians later confirmed the vehicle had no apparent defects.

"When Mrs. Winestone's autopsy results were released, there were no indications of heart attack or stroke, and her blood work showed no signs she'd been impaired by drugs or alcohol."

Abe took a deep breath and nodded at his brother, who continued, "However, that wasn't the only thing her blood confirmed. It held another secret, as did Joseph Winestone's. Her mother's blood type was O and her father's type B, but Victoria's was type AB, meaning they didn't match. Joseph and Susan Winestone couldn't have been her birth parents."

"My blood type is AB, too," I whispered. Leah gave my hand a quick squeeze but motioned for Elijah to continue.

"Victoria was devastated, not only had she tragically lost her parents, but possibly her identity, as well. They had obviously not meant for her to find out she'd been adopted. Being the way she was, Victoria didn't fault them for it. She simply believed they'd had their reasons and the best of intentions. Nevertheless, once she knew, she was determined to find out more about her background.

"Having been an only child, she had no other family to confide in, so she turned to her parent's oldest friend, Sir Edward Harrington. Though he was known as Sir Edward to everyone else, Victoria insisted upon calling him Sir Harry from the time she was a toddler, despite her parent's opposition.

"Anyway, upon their deaths, Sir Edward received a key from Joseph Winestone to a safety deposit box at a bank near his residence in London. The letter that accompanied the key was written in Mr. Winestone's handwriting and instructed Sir Edward to review the contents and make his own decision with regard to their handling. He immediately called Victoria and encouraged her to come to London."

"Did Sir Edward know about Victoria's adoption beforehand?" I asked.

"That's a good question. Victoria asked him the same thing." Abe smiled. "Though the Winestones never directly discussed it with him, he guessed an adoption had taken place. They were very public people, and though there were months they would hunker down to work on a project, a pregnancy would not have gone unnoticed. No one said a word when little Victoria was finally spotted in public. Perhaps because of the era, or perhaps, like Sir Edward, people were happy the couple had something other than work to occupy their lives. As strange as it sounds, the adoption never came up."

"Perhaps the wealthy do live charmed lives," Leah remarked as I excused myself so I could take Nicoh for a quick walk. Poor baby hadn't gotten much attention since introductions were made and had been dancing on the tips of his paws for at least fifteen minutes. He finished his business, and after I gave him some well-deserved scratches, we headed back to join the others.

Preoccupied with the conversation, I hadn't realized how much the patio had filled in. We now had company on both sides: a couple bickering over wedding invites on the left and a guy wearing an Arizona Diamondbacks hat on the right similar to one my dad once owned, listening to his iPod while reading the paper.

I realized Abe and Elijah were laughing at Leah's stories of our good old days in high school, so I quickly sat down and gave her the look, which made them laugh even harder. Great. That was the last time she was going to borrow my vintage 1950s cat-eye sunglasses, which coincidentally, were currently perched on top of her head. Would anyone notice if I suddenly snatched them?

Once the chuckles finally subsided and I decided to leave the sunglasses alone, I nodded at Elijah to continue.

"Victoria went to London to meet Sir Edward. Before opening the safety deposit box, he let her read the letter, in which Joseph Winestone came clean about the adoption. He and his wife had intended to have children, but work encompassed their lives. By the time they felt they could make a go of it, it was too late. Determined to have a family, they did the next best thing. They adopted.

"According to the letter, the box contained the documentation relating to the adoption and as promised, an overwhelming pile of paper was enclosed. The adoption had been arranged through the Sterling Joy Agency, a Chicago-based firm. Neither Sir Edward nor Victoria was familiar with the laws relating to adoptions, but it seemed the Winestones collected every tidbit of information they could find on the birth parents, including age, appearance, education, occupation, current relationship, reason for the adoption, etc., which is how they found out both were deceased.

The birth mother had died of complications following child-birth and the father…passed, a short time later." Elijah swallowed hard. Clearly, something bothered him about that but before I could ask, he went on, "Fortunately, they had the foresight to make arrangements with an agency in the event of their deaths—likely because they had no living family—otherwise their children would have become wards of the state.

"Anyway, Victoria also found out about you. Under a section titled 'Other Children Born to Birth Parents', there was a single listing: 'Female, one-month of age, born at the University of Chicago Medical Center'. Same birth location as was listed for Victoria, as well as her age at the time of her birth.

"This intrigued both Victoria and Sir Edward. Why hadn't her parents adopted both children? They had wanted a family—this would have been the perfect solution. They found the answer further down in the papers.

Once the Winestones learned of the second child—you—they immediately contacted the agency. Though the agency sympa-thized, they claimed the birth parents had explicitly stated under no circumstances were the children to be adopted together. And, based upon the letters exchanged between Sterling Joy and the Winestones, it also became quite clear the agency had been paid handsomely to honor the birth parent's last wishes."

"That is strange," Leah commented, before looking to me to gauge my reaction to this news. I wasn't sure what my face showed, but I was astonished.

"There was one final surprise waiting on the bottom of the security deposit box. Five documents were bound together, almost symbolically. They included Victoria's current birth certificate, her original birth certificate, your original birth certificate, your current birth certificate and your parent's address." My address.

"Oh, my gosh," I gasped as I looked at Leah, flabbergasted, "that is totally insane. Do you think they contacted my parents— that my parents knew?"

"We don't know, AJ," Abe replied quietly, "and with the players deceased, I'm not sure we'll ever know. It was this information, however, that prompted Victoria to search for you. And, it was at the beginning of this search she learned of your parent's tragic accident. That's when she hired us."

Leah murmured absently, "Perhaps there's another safety deposit box lurking around somewhere? One with more clues?"

"We'd thought of that too. It's certainly something we can pursue," Elijah replied, "but first, there's a bit more we need to tell you."

"Are you serious?" Leah squawked a bit too loudly, which made Nicoh moan like a moose.

I couldn't blame him, I wanted to moan like a moose myself —this conversation was becoming more and more like the one with Ramirez. Abe and Elijah both apologized, but I told them to continue, so Abe picked up where Elijah had left off.

"When Victoria got back from London, she went to her parent's house to check on things. On the answering machine, there was a message from someone at the dealership where her mother had purchased her Jaguar, apologizing for the mix-up and confirming she still wanted the original car. Victoria lost it."

"What rock had this guy been living under?" Leah snarked.

"Victoria said she gave him an earful," Abe replied. "The manager apologized profusely. He returned from a cruise vacation and wasn't exactly sure how it happened, but in his absence, the assistant manager had delivered her mother's custom-designed car to another client. Rather than disappoint that client, who had already fallen in love with the car, he immediately called Victoria's mother to confess his oversight. As gracious as ever, she let the assistant manager off the hook and agreed to take the car until another could be ordered."

"So, the car she was driving when the accident occurred wasn't the car she should have been driving?" I asked.

"Nope," Abe continued, "but that wasn't the end of it."

"Of course not," I retorted, perhaps a bit too sarcastically, "why would it be?"

"What raised the red flags—and frankly, still raises the hair on the back our necks—was when Victoria asked to speak with the assistant manager."

"The manager had already fired him?" Leah asked.

"He probably should have been fired, but no, it didn't go down quite that way," Abe replied. "He disappeared."

"Well, perhaps that's not such a loss," I countered.

"No, probably not," Abe agreed, "but when he went missing, so did all the other client's paperwork."

"As if that weren't a flaming red flag," Leah mused. This situation just kept getting better and better.

"So, is that something you'd still be willing to look into?" I asked, not even remotely familiar with the private investigator protocol, considering Victoria had originally hired them.

"Absolutely," Abe and Elijah said at the same time. Unless I was mistaken, they almost seemed relieved I had asked. Perhaps my affirmation meant they had passed some sort of imaginary test?

"Well, I'm sure your brains are mush by now, we've covered so much stuff today." Elijah smiled warmly. "Maybe now would be a good time to discuss where we go from here, if that's what you'd like?"

Though I was pretty sure he was asking me, Leah nearly swooned as she burst out, "We definitely like." I rewarded her by smacking her arm, which drew chuckles from Abe and Elijah and a serious unhappy-face from Leah.

"Yeah, I think so," I replied as Leah feigned rubbing her injured limb, "but I'm not sure how we do this. Do we divide and conquer, or do you guys prefer to work solo?"

"Heck, no, we'll take any help we can get, plus, we've got Anna too, who has pretty much already made this case her mission in life," Abe commented.

"Wow," was all I could muster. Victoria must have had as profound of an effect on Anna as she had on Abe and Elijah. In my opinion, they all seemed pretty loyal to the cause.

"So, if you are cool with it, here's what we thought some of the next steps—or action items as we call them—could be," Elijah said.

"Oooh, I like action items," Leah cooed but toned her oozing enthusiasm down once she caught a glimpse of my I-will-smack-you-again look.

"As I was saying," Elijah stifled another laugh, obviously enjoying our banter, "if you wouldn't be opposed to it, it would be helpful if you could find out some more information about the adoption, about your biological parents, their backgrounds, etc. We'll have Anna send you the documents Victoria brought back from the London safety deposit box."

At my questioning look, he continued, "Victoria would have wanted you to have them. I know she would." Elijah turned to his brother, who nodded in agreement.

I nodded back. "I can definitely do that. Plus, as the adoptee, it would probably be easier for me to obtain the information, without raising a ruckus."

"Yeah, we'd prefer it if you limited the ruckus-raising. We wouldn't want it to result in a brew-ha-ha, after all," Abe teased. "Anyway, while you look into that, we'll try to find out more about the dealership's missing assistant manager and the client who took possession of Mrs. Winestone's Jag.

"In addition, we'll be tracking down whatever information Victoria found that led her to believe your parent's plane crash was not an accident," Elijah said. I had almost forgotten about the cryptic voicemail Victoria had left Abe and Elijah. Her last voicemail.

"She believed 'bigger forces were at play' that affected all of us," I repeated from memory, my voice barely a whisper.

Elijah nodded. "We're not stopping until we determine what those forces might be. Whatever they are, they killed Victoria."

* * *

"Well, there's good news and bad news." Leah sighed as we walked to the parking lot several minutes later.

"Bad news first, as always," I told her, though I wasn't sure I was prepared for anymore.

"The bad news is they didn't pull up in a red Ferrari." She pouted, confirming my previous suspicions about the dual *Magnum, PI* fantasy. Stupefied, I could only shake my head.

"But, the good news is—it was black!" She squealed with delight.

More proof that the more things change, the more they stay the same. With the month I'd had so far, I guess I should have taken comfort in that.

CHAPTER TEN

He sat with his back to them. Arizona Diamondbacks baseball hat pulled low, eyes covered by dark aviator sunglasses.

Their conversation barely amused him.

Amateurs.

What did intrigue him was the girl. She was a dead ringer for the other one. Perhaps she would be just as feisty.

He could hardly wait to find out.

CHAPTER ELEVEN

After meeting with Abe and Elijah, all I wanted to do was take a nap. My brain hurt and I needed to put it into neutral for a while. Unfortunately, I had Charlie's project to complete, preferably before he burst a gasket. I always carried photo equipment in the back of my Mini Cooper, so I dropped Leah off at her office and headed over to his condo in Tempe.

I wasn't sure if his intention for showcasing the condo in the local home decor magazine was to sell it or to show it off—it was always a bit of a toss-up with Charlie—but my guess was the latter. Either way, the deadline for the winter edition was fast approaching, which had him chomping at the bit.

The editor offered to send one of her staff photographers over, but for as much of a braggart as Charlie was, he despised having people touch his stuff. After rebuking the idea of using one of the magazine's photographers—huffily exclaiming he had one of his own—Charlie promptly texted me and demanded I contact the editor as soon as possible, or else.

I did but found myself apologizing to her for half an hour for Charlie's rudeness before she agreed to send me the magazine's specs. I continued to grovel and was granted three days to submit the photos, though I knew the deadline was at least twenty days out. Deciding not to press my luck, I thanked her profusely and hung up, feeling about as well-received as a piece of gum on the bottom of her Jimmy Choos.

Thankfully, I was on the short of list of people he considered worthy of granting entry to his condo, though I was convinced his preference was to have me suit up like the forensics team on CSI. Fortunately, he settled for powder- and latex-free gloves and elasticized, non-static booties. Yeah, don't even get me started. Of course, I was required to leave Nicoh with the doorman, who always had a few extra doggie treats handy.

Sufficiently geared up, I was ready to go in. The condo had an open floor plan—reminiscent of the lofts you might see in Manhattan—and was designed in an ultra-modern industrial style —lots of steel and glass. Charlie furnished it with more steel and glass, using only black, gray and an occasional splash of white to accent the space. It was kind of cool, in a very sterile, antiseptic way. Case in point, his floor was definitely cleaner than any plate in my house.

I was grateful Charlie couldn't be present while I worked. His personal assistant, Arch, was there in his place to hawk-eye my every move. I actually preferred him to Charlie and found him fairly harmless, though I was pretty sure I spotted him snapping pictures of me with his iPhone. Whatever—I could deal with Arch.

I took several shots on both levels of the condo—the natural lighting was awesome—and was able to capture what I needed within a couple of hours. I packed my gear and shouted goodbye to Arch, though I knew he was lurking somewhere nearby. I collected Nicoh from the doorman, who had been receiving the royal treatment in my absence. Still, he trotted happily to the Mini and jumped into the passenger seat.

As we drove home, I suddenly realized how tired I was. Typically, Leah mused at my Energizer-bunny intensity, but the events of the day had drained me, both physically and emotionally. My mind hadn't gotten the signal, there was so much to contemplate.

I decided to wait for the package from Abe and Elijah's assistant, Anna, to begin my part of the research. Instead, I called Ramirez to give him an update, though I knew he wasn't anticipating one. He must have been expecting another call because he answered on the first ring, but seemed genuinely pleased to hear from me and listened quietly as I filled him in on the meeting with Abe and Elijah.

Only when I finished did he speak, "How are you, AJ?"

"I don't know. I've got a lot to digest and yet, I just want to sleep. Unfortunately, my mind won't let me."

"I'm sorry, perhaps I shouldn't have pushed you?"

"Hey, Victoria died trying to make contact with me. I owe it to her to figure this out, to finish it, whatever *it* is."

Ramirez was silent for a moment then quietly said, "I'm here for you, AJ, day or night."

"Thanks, Detective."

"Jonah, please call me Jonah."

"Thanks, Jonah. Have a good night."

"You're welcome, AJ. Sleep well."

I appreciated the sentiment but doubted rest would come anytime soon. And yet, I was out as soon as my head hit the pillow.

CHAPTER TWELVE

The documentation from the safety deposit box arrived promptly at 10 a.m. via Federal Express. Anna called less than a minute after I signed for the package to confirm it had arrived. I told her it had and thanked her for her promptness in sending it.

"Have Abe and Elijah made it back to L.A.?" I asked.

"Not yet, but I expect them this afternoon," Anna replied.

"Please, thank them again for me. I truly appreciate everything."

"Thank you, for agreeing to help. We all liked Victoria and hope that while getting you some much-needed answers, we'll also get her the justice she deserves."

"I hope I can find something that will help. By the way, my friend Leah has also offered to assist if she can. I probably should have mentioned it yesterday, but she's a reporter, so she has some resources and connections that might be useful."

Anna's laugh tinkled into the phone, a pleasant, carefree sound. "We're well aware of Ms. Campbell's profession. And please, thank her for us. We may need to utilize some of those resources in the future."

Despite being busted, I decided to play it cool. "Uh, great. I'll let her know," I stammered, making Anna laugh again. Being cool under pressure was so underrated.

"And AJ, I'm a resource, too, should you need one."

"Thanks, Anna, I appreciate it. I have a feeling I'm going to need all the help I can get."

"Just remember, we are always here for you, AJ." I truly believed she meant it.

We said our goodbyes and hung up. Even though I was left sitting with the FedEx envelope, thanks to Anna's call, I didn't feel so alone.

I still wasn't sure I was up for the task at hand, but with Charlie's photos already e-mailed to the magazine, Nicoh snoring soundly on his doggie pillow in the living room and a full caramel sauce latte sitting in front of me, I'd run out of reasons to procrastinate. Unceremoniously, I opened the FedEx box from Anna.

On the top of the stack, she had left a note indicating all documents from the safety deposit box were present and ordered by date. I wondered if they'd been like that or if Anna had arranged them for efficiency. Either way, I was appreciative. Just looking at the size of the stack was daunting enough, without having to organize it as well. It was official—Anna was my new second best friend.

Following Anna's letter was Joseph Winestone's letter to Sir Edward. It matched what Elijah had mentioned the previous day. Winestone had come clean to his old friend about the adoption and the supporting documents contained within the safety deposit box.

Four to five reams of adoption-related legalese comprised the bulk of the documentation. I waded through it, though I needed an interpreter—and a stronger beverage—to understand it all. I did make note of the pertinent stuff I found: the address and phone numbers of 1) the primary contact at the Sterling Joy Agency, Mrs.

Mavis Baumgardner, 2) the Winestone's lawyer, Mr. Jonathan Silverton and 3) the contact at the University of Chicago Medical Center, Cheryl Earley. After nearly thirty years, I wondered how current this information was going to be. My guess was not very.

Next was a document titled "Non-identifying Information." Interesting, considering while it didn't provide names of the birth parents, etc., it certainly seemed to provide a lot of other personal information. In fact, it was more information than most people probably knew about me. I read through it anyway, to see if anything stood out.

Non-identifying Information

Age: Father—35; Mother—34

Race: Both—Caucasian

Religion: Unknown

Ethnic background: Unknown

General description: Father—6 feet 2 inches, 210 pounds, black-brown hair, dark-blue eyes; Mother—5 feet 10 inches, 130 pounds, reddish-brown hair, blue-gray eyes

Education: Both—Post-graduate; Father—PhD

Occupation: Father—Scientist; Mother—Researcher

Hobbies: Unknown

Interests: Unknown

Talents: Both—multilingual; specific languages unknown

Relationship between birth parents (*Married, Single, Separated, Divorced*): Unknown

Birth grandparents: Deceased/Unknown

Current status/Reason given for adoption: Birth parents deceased

Actual birthplace and date of adoptee:
University of Chicago Medical Center, Chicago, Illinois; June 19

Age of adoptee at time of adoption: Two months

Existence and age of other children born to birth parents:
One; Girl—Two months

Current status of other children: Unknown

That was it for the non-identifying information. Next was a letter from Joseph Winestone to Mavis Baumgardner, requesting additional information about the parents' deaths, as well as an updated status of the other baby girl.

Mrs. Baumgardner must have initially elected not to respond in writing because the following pages were handwritten notes—perhaps by Mr. Winestone—detailing a conversation between Mrs. Baumgardner, Jonathan Silverton and the Winestones that addressed the previous letter.

The notes were consistent with the information Elijah had supplied the previous day regarding the arrangements made by the biological parents and the subsequent passing of the mother following childbirth. And then, the bombshell Elijah hadn't shared.

According to the notes, the father committed suicide shortly after his twin girls were born and the mother of his children had died. My heart ached as my eyes filled with tears. I dropped the papers, hugged my knees and rocked back and forth.

Sufficiently subdued, I returned to my task. Mrs. Baumgardner had chosen not to share any more information regarding the suicide, though perhaps no one had asked. Would that have been considered tacky? If so, I would have flunked in the social etiquette arena, but then I didn't feel so crummy because I knew Leah would have too.

For now, I appreciated a reprieve from the details, but it was information we'd have to follow up on regardless. I made a mental note to add that to the list later, on Leah's side. I understood why Elijah had hesitated yesterday and silently thanked him for his compassion.

According to Mr. Winestone's notes, Mrs. Baumgardner indicated the birth parents had made it abundantly clear that under no circumstances were the children to be adopted together. Though the Winestones were clearly disappointed, Mrs. Baumgardner refused to be pressed further on the topic. There wasn't much merit in the rest of their conversation, though Mr. Winestone did make a note to follow up on the girl at a later date.

Sure enough, immediately following Mr. Winestone's hand-written notes were a slew of letters, both to and from Mrs. Baumgardner that continued to breach the subject. She remained unrelenting—under no circumstances would she violate the agreement the agency had made with the birth parents. In her final letter, however, she did assure the Wine-stones the other baby girl had found a loving home, though she shared no more than that. In my book, the whole thing felt off somehow.

Finally, I reached the birth certificates—the documents I dreaded, and yet longed to see. I was glad Abe and Elijah had prepared me for this, but my stomach was still filled with butterflies.

I carefully lifted Victoria's most-recent birth certificate out and found mine directly beneath. Though both contained facts I already knew, I was shaking. Where the heck had the Winestones gotten this information? I shuddered, considering the possibilities. Next was a plain piece of typing paper, which contained nothing but my parent's Phoenix address, now my home. Though I'd been told it was here, I had hoped for some note, some comment or indication of how it had made its way into the Winestone's possession. If it had secrets to tell—which I was sure it did—it wasn't sharing.

I knew the final two pieces of paper contained the most important information—perhaps more important than anything I would read again. I took a deep breath and grasped a certificate in each hand. As I held them side-by-side, I read the names of the birth parents I would never know: Father—Martin Alexander Singer; Mother—Alison Marie Anders.

I then proceeded to read the name of each child. Ella Marie Singer was born at 2:15:30 a.m. on June 19. Victoria had been my older sister by a minute and a half, I realized as I glanced at the other certificate. Arianna Elena Singer had been born at 2:17:00 a.m. on the same day. The butterflies turned to outright queasiness as I absorbed the fact my parents—Richard and Eileen Jackson— had kept all but the surname I'd been given at birth. How much more had they known, I wondered? And, had it played a role in their deaths? Victoria thought it had, and she'd only begun to unravel the secrets.

Well, big sister, I thought as I gently placed our birth certificates back into the box. It's high time we finished what you started.

CHAPTER THIRTEEN

I was jacked-up and ready to roll. I decided to start my action items by contacting the individuals and organizations involved with the adoption. First on my list was Mavis Baumgardner of the Sterling Joy Agency. I used the phone number from the documentation in the Winestone's safety deposit box and received a "number is no longer in service" recording, so I called directory assistance. There was no listing under the Sterling Joy Agency, Mavis Baumgardner or any Baumgardner, for that matter, in Chicago or any of the surrounding areas. Perhaps they moved out of the state? It wouldn't be all that surprising, considering it had been almost thirty years.

I searched the Internet, and while there was no listing or website for the agency, I did find a tidbit in a twenty-five-year-old business journal-type article that read "…Maxwell Baumgardner and his wife, Mavis, founders of the Sterling Joy Agency, have decided to close their doors after years of service to the community. When interviewed, Mr. Baumgardner indicated the decision had been based on the desire to spend more time with family and to pursue other opportunities."

I wondered what those "other opportunities" might have been, so I continued my search. Two hours later, I had nothing. Nada. It appeared as though the Baumgardners had fallen off the face of the earth. I said appeared, not had. I had one more trick up my sleeve—a crack-shot newspaper reporter and researcher extraordinaire—my BFF, Leah. I started a to-do list for her. Generous of me, I know. Seriously, the girl lives for the stuff.

Next on my list was Jonathan Silverton, the Winestone's former lawyer. This time, the number worked, however, I awkwardly learned he had passed a few years earlier after suffering a massive stroke. His widow, Jeannie, was remarkably pleasant, and though I was somewhat vague about my reason for calling, seemed happy to have a distraction from her shows.

She had heard about the Winestone's accident on the national news and apologized for my loss. Ok, I *might* have told her I was Victoria's sister, but she drew her own conclusion about my relationship to the Winestones.

According to Mrs. Silverton, her husband had been in private practice for the better part of his career, though she made no mention of the Sterling Joy Agency. I asked if she knew what had become of his case files, and she said no. I believed her. She was probably one of those wives who had no idea what their husbands did during the day and didn't care to know, just as long as they came home for dinner. Now, I'm not saying there's anything wrong with that, it just wouldn't work for me. *Disclaimer:* This is solely the opinion of a single woman in her late twenties—please feel free to draw your own conclusions.

Anyway, as it was clearly a dead-end, I thanked the nice lady for her time, and we said our goodbyes. It wasn't all for nothing. I did come up with some nice to-dos for Anna's list. Yup, still spreading the generosity.

Before contacting the University of Chicago Medical Center, I did some quick research. Cheryl Earley had been an administrator at the time Victoria and I were born. Turns out, she still was, but nowadays, she was a little higher up on the food chain.

Unfortunately, in my experience, the higher up you are, the more assistants there are between you and Jill Public, aka me. As expected, it took me quite a few transfers to get to the point where I was granted access to Ms. Earley's voicemail.

Imagine my surprise when Cheryl Earley picked up. Avoiding the crazy, sordid details, I stuck with the basics and told Ms. Earley I was trying to track down information surrounding my adoption—that my sister and I had been born at UCMC almost thirty years earlier and both of our parents had died a short time later, resulting in our adoptions with a local agency. I was about to go on, but she stopped me dead in my tracks.

"Oh my goodness," she whispered, "you're one of the twins."

"You know about me?" I croaked. "About my family?"

"I could hardly forget. I had recently been promoted to my first administrator position. You and your sister had been born prematurely—by a couple of weeks if I remember correctly—but you were both healthy. And your mother, she was doing great. Then, all of a sudden, she wasn't. She went so fast. They couldn't save her…" she trailed off. "I'm sorry. I shouldn't be telling you this."

"No, no…please, it's why I called." I told her of my adoptive parent's deaths, Victoria's—then Ella—parent's deaths and finally, about Victoria's murder.

I waited for her response. And waited. Then, I realized I'd made a colossal error in judgment. I was convinced she was going to hang up on me.

Instead, she surprised me. "Arianna, I'm so sorry, for all the loss you've had to endure. If only things could have been differ-ent. It's almost as though your mother's death set off a chain reac-tion that would follow you for the rest of your life." I would later reflect on the truth of that statement. "What can I do to help?"

"I'm still trying to get my head around all of this. I've run into nothing but brick walls so far, but perhaps you can help me find out more information about my birth parents—any documents, records, etc. that might still exist. Anything, no matter how insignificant it seems, could lead to something."

"Please dear, call me Cheryl. I think I can help. Records dating back that far are archived at an understaffed, off-site facility. It's going to take some time, but I might have a way to cut through some of the bureaucratic red tape. Here's what we'll do—give me your e-mail address."

After I rattled off my email, she continued, "I'm going to e-mail you the standard medical record request form. Just fill out the basic parts and e-mail it back to me, along with a copy of your current birth certificate and driver's license. Once I've got it, I'll fill in all the nitty-gritty details—with the appropriate codes—so you get anything and everything related to your parents. Believe me, when I'm done, if one of your birth parents broke a foot and had it casted here when they were twelve-years-old, you'll know about it." I chuckled.

"Anyway, I know the director over there. He owes me a favor. I'll call and give him a heads-up, then send a messenger to place the request and your documents right into his hands. When his people are done, I'll have him do the same back to me, and I'll ship it to you overnight. Will that work, Arianna?"

"Heck, yes. Th-thank you," I stammered, before attempting to collect my wits. "A couple of questions, though?"

Cheryl laughed. "Shoot."

"Don't take this the wrong way, Cheryl, but why are you helping me? Aren't you risking a lot?"

Again, she laughed, but perhaps a bit more tersely. "Call me jaded. Or perhaps I've become too complacent over the years, but it's been a long time since I've had the opportunity to the right thing for the right reasons. And this feels right. Plus, you caught me on a good day." It was my turn to chuckle.

"Whatever the reasons, thank you, again. This means a lot to me."

"I know it does. You said a 'couple' of questions?"

"Oh yeah, please call me AJ? All of my friends do."

"Certainly, AJ. I'd like to hear how this turns out."

As promised, I had an e-mail from Cheryl waiting in my Inbox shortly after the call ended. I quickly filled out the section she'd highlighted, scanned my birth certificate and driver's license and e-mailed them back with another quick thank you.

I know I should have been ecstatic following the call with Cheryl —a part of me was—but I also worried it would lead to more questions. What is it they say about not looking a gift horse in the mouth? Perhaps said horse should just kick my butt now and be done with it.

While I'd been talking to Cheryl, Anna had emailed Sir Edward Harrington's home and cell phone numbers and indicated she'd given him a head's up—he would be expecting my call—so I kept it to the basics, leaving him enough of a message on his cell to elicit a return call.

After that, I took a couple of minutes to jot down a few to-do items I'd conjured up for Anna, Leah and myself throughout the day. I decided to wait until I heard back from Sir Edward before touching base with them regarding these items, just in case I needed to add a few more.

LEAH

Maxwell & Mavis Baumgardner / Sterling Joy Agency

Question: What happened to the Sterling Joy Agency?

Question: What "other opportunities" did the Baumgardners have in mind?

Question: What became of the couple?

Martin Singer / Bio dad

Question: Are there other details surrounding his suicide?

ANNA

Jonathan Silverton / Winestone's lawyer

Question: What happened to Silverton's files once he retired?

Question: Who are the Winestone's other lawyers?

Question: Did the other lawyers know about Silverton?

Question: Did Silverton procure the birth certificates and/or my parent's address at the Winestone's request (provided they did not come from the Baumgardners)?

AJ

Sir Edward Harrington / Winestone family friend

Question: Did he know Jonathan Silverton?

Question: Did the Winestones know my parents?

Cheryl Earley / UCMC Administrator

Awaiting records on Martin Singer and Alison Anders / bio parents

Other

Question: Did the birth certificates and/or my parent's address come from the Baumgardners, despite Mrs. Baumgardner's resolve to the contrary (provided they did not come from Silverton)?

Once completed, I reviewed my to-do items and chuckled as I flashed on a quote from Nero Wolfe to Archie Goodwin, "...I didn't say this [exercise] *would* be useful, only that it *could* be useful..."

At this point, I could only hope Abe, Elijah and Anna were faring better.

CHAPTER FOURTEEN

Meanwhile, Abe and Elijah were wondering the same thing about AJ.

They had returned to L.A. the previous day, ready to hit the ground running. Unfortunately, the only things they managed to hit in the past several hours were a series of brick walls.

Victoria had been convinced the Jackson's plane crash was not accidental. They learned from working long, hard hours with her she didn't jump to conclusions easily—quite the opposite, in fact —and oh, so stubborn, that one. She routinely drove them crazy with her don't-tell-me-prove-it-to-me attitude. And yet, the day before she was killed, she'd been so certain, despite the fact they had previously gone over and over the official report, talked to the crash investigator, looked at the crash site and found nothing. What had changed her mind?

While she had likely memorized the contents of the report, Abe and Elijah agreed it couldn't have been the source of her new evidence. Anna had locked their only copy in the safe weeks ago, and Victoria hadn't asked her to retrieve it or make copies. They all agreed she would have done so, had it contained the linchpin they'd spent months searching for. As simple as an explanation as that seemed, it was her nature. She simply wouldn't have made the comment without having evidence to support it. They'd already searched her condo and had come up empty.

That left Winslow Clark, the crash investigator. Surely, she must have contacted him and asked him to confirm some nugget of information? Their disappointment mounted when he said no, not only had he not talked to Victoria, he hadn't seen her since the three of them had met him at the crash site several months earlier. He didn't ask about her, and they didn't offer—no need to voluntarily put her death out there—so once they had their answer, they thanked Clark for his time and hung up.

Too frustrated to think straight, they headed back to the office to touch base with Anna. She was not only an amazing admin, she got them back on track when they went off the rails. Yup, right now they needed a strong dose of Anna.

Anna was delighted to see them again, too. She knew the Phoenix trip had taken its toll—especially after learning of Victoria's death—but she had also seen grief and anger turn into something else—a mission. It had become personal. For all of them. She smiled warmly as they bounded through the door, like two schoolboys fresh off the playground. They scooped her up into a big bear hug and spun her around, laughing as they ignored her feigned pleas about wrinkling her outfit. Finally, Abe put her back on her feet, but not before Elijah mock-mussed her hair.

"Touch the locks and you're done, buster," she growled, though there was a gleam of mischief in her eyes. She made a display of smoothing the wrinkles out of the black long sleeve cotton blouse she'd paired with rolled-up boyfriend jeans and ballet flats, but a grin peeked out from under the long raven hair that had fallen over her face during their horseplay.

Abe and Elijah laughed heartily. Though she was drop-dead gorgeous—easily passing as a sibling of Angie Everhart's—and as sweet as they come, she could definitely throw-down when she needed to. Growing up with five older brothers would do that to a girl. Plus, they'd seen her in action at a couple of her martial arts classes. Anna wasn't a gal you'd want to mess with in a dark alley, much less a well-lit one. Of course, she'd lay you out flat, then apologize by baking you fudge brownies later. Still, they were glad Anna was on their side.

"Any word from AJ?" Elijah asked her.

"Yeah, in fact, we've spoken on the phone, as well as e-mailed back and forth a few times. She's busy tracking down leads at the hospital and adoption agency and is also hoping to speak person-ally with Jonathan Silverton and Sir Edward," Anna replied. "Oh, and she fessed-up about her friend Leah." They all laughed, before she added, "Anyway, I like her. She's got spunk and isn't afraid to speak her mind."

"Kind of like you, huh? Like two beans on a stalk," Abe chuckled as he went into the kitchenette to fill his water bottle.

"That's two peas in a pod, smart guy!" Anna shouted at him.

"Thanks for proving my point," he shouted back, laughing.

Elijah took his brother's absence to lean in and whisper, "I think Abe has a little crush on AJ."

"Really?" Anna replied, crooking her eyebrow. Elijah nodded and put a finger to his lips as Abe returned.

"What are you two whispering about?" he asked, eyeing them both suspiciously. "You know my birthday isn't until next month, though if you wanted to start shopping now, there's a sweeeet Jag—"

"Stop right there," Anna teased, "you'll ruin the big surprise." Roars of laughter filled the office.

Once the last of the chuckles subsided, Elijah turned the conversation back to the case, "Speaking of Jags, we should follow up with the dealership manager about his missing employee."

"And the missing paperwork," Abe added.

"Let me go grab his number out of the file, and we'll conference him," Elijah said.

As he strode into the other office, Abe turned to Anna and murmured, "I think Elijah has a crush on AJ."

"You don't say?" Anna deadpanned.

As Elijah came back, file in hand, Abe gave her a sly wink, to which she returned a quick nod. His secret was safe with her.

Oblivious to their collusion, Elijah sat down and dialed the dealership's number. The receptionist transferred the call directly to the manager, who picked up on the first ring.

"Jaguar of Malibu, Paul Switzer at your service. Today is the day—don't just dream it—drive it!"

He deflated a bit when Elijah introduced himself as a PI—most likely after mentally calculating the probability of a sale—but allowed Elijah to continue.

"My brother, Abe, and my associate, Anna are also on the call with us," he paused as they said quick hellos. "Victoria Winestone hired us several months ago on another matter. It has recently come to our attention, however, the situation with her mother's car might be related to this matter, so we're hoping you would entertain a few questions?"

"I have already explained everything to Victoria," Switzer huffed, "as well as to the police. Three times."

"If you wouldn't mind telling us, just once, we'd greatly appreciate it," Anna added in her most sultry voice. Perhaps a feminine touch would inspire cooperation? It did. Abe and Elijah rolled their eyes as Anna smirked.

"This 'situation,' as you so kindly phrased it, started when I won the dealership's yearly raffle for a European cruise. First time in twenty years I could take the wife on a real vacation. And this happens. Worse cluster in my entire career and it goes down the minute I walk out of the dealership." His frustration oozed through the phone.

"My now-former assistant manager, Tanner Dolby, was supposed to be in charge during my absence. Ms. Winestone's car was delivered on a truck, along with four others, as scheduled. Her car was the only one that had been a custom job. You know—special wheels, tires, leather, etc.—the works. The color was the same as one of the other four, but even then, you'd have to be a complete idiot to confuse the two, which Dolby managed to do.

"Dolby delivered Mrs. Winestone's car to another customer, Frederick Glass, before realizing his mistake. He claimed to have called Glass back immediately, but Glass rebuffed him, indicating his wife had already fallen in love with her new car. Under no circumstances was he prepared to disappoint her because of Dolby's oversight.

"Rather than get me involved, Dolby contacted Mrs. Winestone himself and played the sympathy card, appealing to her good nature. She was legendary for it, but he took advantage of her generosity as a means of covering for his mistake. It disgusts me to think about it, especially considering I will never get a chance to make it right with her," he sighed, his former employee's manipulation obviously weighed heavily on his conscience.

"Anyway, Dolby convinced Mrs. Winestone to take Glass' Jag temporarily—still a remarkable piece of machinery, just not what she'd ordered and paid for—while he ordered another customized car. I can't believe she went for it. It had taken months to get the car in, not to mention the weeks she'd already put into carefully selecting the customizations. Once she agreed, he probably figured the problem was solved, and he was off the hook."

"So he confessed when you got back and *then* bailed?" Abe asked.

Switzer laughed harshly. "Nope, I didn't even get the courtesy. He bolted the day Mrs. Winestone took delivery of the car—originally Glass' car—and never came back. My sales manager didn't have the good sense to call me while it was going down, so I got hit with everything my first day back from vacation. Let's just say, the only one I plan on taking in the future is called retirement."

"Victoria mentioned that when Dolby went missing, Glass' paperwork did too?" Elijah asked.

"Ha, I wish it was only the paperwork. Dolby not only allegedly removed or destroyed the relevant physical documentation but the electronic stuff, as well. And, believe me, it wasn't like you see on *CSI* or *Law & Order* when they are able to retrieve traces of the deleted documents after twenty minutes. In this real-life scenario, the hard drive was g-o-n-e, as in Dolby swapped it out with a new one and took it with him. Allegedly, of course.

"Anyway, I haven't even told you the best part yet. After Dolby skipped out, Mrs. Winestone's custom car went missing. And Frederick Glass? Well, he never existed."

Abe, Elijah, and Anna looked at one another. Something wasn't adding up. "Seems like a pretty elaborate plan just to steal a car," Anna commented, to no one in particular. "Why the cover-up? Why not just take Mrs. Winestone's car and go? Unless…" she paused as they all mentally finished her thought. Dolby needed to get the other car into Mrs. Winestone's hands. They were silent as they pondered the possibilities.

It was Switzer who finally spoke, changing the subject. "Say, you guys mind doing me a favor? Would you let Victoria know she left her sunglasses here? I would have mailed them, but I don't know where she lives."

"Wait, Victoria was there?" Anna stuttered as Abe and Elijah's eyes widened in surprise. "When was this?"

"Um, a couple of weeks ago," Switzer replied. "I needed her to come down and finalize some paperwork pertaining to her mother's car, for insurance purposes and things of that nature."

"We always assumed she had only called you," Abe

commented, looking at Anna and his brother, who both nodded in return.

"Well, she did call me, but that was on a previous occasion, after my new assistant manager left a message on her parent's machine about her mother's car. He's not from around here and, unfortunately, wasn't aware they'd been killed several months prior.

"Anyway, on the day she was here, I had to leave her for a couple of minutes while I dealt with a crisis in the service department. When I came back, she was gone. The receptionist, Bonnie, said Victoria literally ran out the door, indicating something urgent had come up, and she was sorry, but she had to leave. Bonnie also said if she hadn't known better, she would have thought Victoria had seen a ghost."

Abe, Elijah, and Anna could do nothing but look at each other, open-mouthed, as Switzer dropped that bombshell.

"Anyway, it must have been something important, because she left some pretty nice Dolce & Gabbana sunglasses behind."

Important indeed.

CHAPTER FIFTEEN

As they looked at one another, an executive decision was made. Elijah gently told Switzer of Victoria's untimely and very recent death. He was quiet for so long, they weren't sure if he had abandoned them altogether.

His voice was somber when he spoke, "I can't believe it." Again, he went silent.

"The thing is, Paul," Abe said, calling the man by his first name, "Victoria was on to something before she was killed. It's a long, convoluted story, but in her last voicemail, she said she had proof her family member's deaths hadn't been accidental," he paused to look at Elijah and Anna.

They nodded, realizing he was being purposely vague with Switzer—throwing out enough rope for him to grasp—without being completely untruthful or divulging too much. They both nodded and made gestures with their hands for him to proceed.

"We had worked together for months, coming up with a lot of facts and theories, but no concrete proof, like you mentioned before. Then suddenly, she meets with you and walks—no, runs —out with what might have been the needle in the haystack, because right after that, she left us that ominous last voicemail.

The next day, she was found…murdered. You get what I'm saying here, Paul?"

Switzer let out a low whistle before replying, "I do, and I get that you're giving me enough to read between the lines." When there was a pregnant pause on the other end, he chuckled. "I may sell cars for a living, but I'm no dolt. I'm good at reading people and situations, even over the phone." That garnered him a collective chuckle. "However," he continued, "I'm not sure what you are asking of me. I mean, if you want to come down and look around, all you need to do is ask."

Anna was the one to breach the silence from their side of the line, "Paul, have you ever considered a job in private investigation?"

An ear-splitting collection of male laughter erupted before he responded, "If I do, I'll let you know." More laughter followed. "So, when can I expect you?" Switzer asked.

"We'll be there in an hour and a half," Elijah responded.

"And guys?" Switzer said. "Make sure you bring back-up."

Abe and Elijah grinned at Anna, who sweetly replied, "Honey, I'll be there."

Still chuckling, they signed-off and piled into Anna's massive SUV. Abe and Elijah speculated loudly as to how she managed to park the thing, to which she tartly replied, "Oh my, I think I accidentally ran over one of your 'toys' while scootching into my parking space this morning. Thought the Ferrari was a speed bump. Sorry, my bad." At their looks of horror, she giggled slyly. Still, they might have been a little bit afraid. Yeah, just a little.

Their kidding continued all the way to Malibu, which made for a quick trip as they pulled into the parking lot of the dealership. Switzer must have been watching for them, because a little round man who could have passed for Hercule Poirot's double, sans the curly-tips on the mustache, was at Anna's door before she had finished parking.

"Holy crap," he exclaimed, "with all the money you've spent buying gas for this tank, you could have bought one of these." He pointed to the sparkling new Jaguars that spanned the front of the lot.

"Yeah, and I could have had a V-8, too," Anna retorted.

"I like this gal," the little man replied as he stuck out a beefy hand. "I'm Paul Switzer. You must be Anna."

She took his hand. "Good guess, now I'm convinced you were meant for PI work." They all laughed as introductions were officially made.

"So, how do you want to do this?" Switzer asked.

"Why don't we walk through your conversation with Victoria. Where you were, what you did," Abe suggested.

"That's easy," Switzer said as he escorted them into the dealership. They nodded at the receptionist at the entrance of the showroom—who must have been Bonnie—before moving into a spacious glass office behind her desk. Nice, if you were into the whole fishbowl theme.

"We were in here until I left to deal with the service issue."

"Did anyone stop by during that time?" Elijah asked.

"No, no one. All the salespeople were with customers."

"What about the service people? You said there was an issue?" Abe added.

"The service manager called me from his office. He didn't stop by."

"What about when you left?" Anna asked.

"I checked with Bonnie, and she said, no, there was no one. And as you can see, from the position of her desk"—it was literally at the entrance of the dealership—"nobody's getting by her without her seeing them. And before you ask, she didn't go on break that entire time.

"Also, not that she was being nosy or anything, but Bonnie

didn't see her take any phone calls. In fact, she said she never saw her pull out a cell, even to check text messages."

"That definitely sounds like Victoria," Elijah commented. "She wasn't one to obsessively check for messages. And she never sent texts."

He turned to his brother and Anna, who were both looking intently at the wall outside Switzer's office.

"What is that?" he asked Switzer as he joined them.

"Oh, that's our employee bulletin board. We post employee accolades, upcoming activities and contests, photos from holiday parties, stuff like that. In fact, you two are looking at the photos from last year's Christmas party. Pretty random stuff, but a fun time for friends and family."

Random was right—there were photos of adults and children of all shapes and sizes eating, dancing, singing or playing games.

"What was here?" Anna asked, pointing to a section of the collage where the construction paper backing peeked through, exposing a small piece of transparent tape.

"Wow, I don't know. Looks like someone pulled one of the photos down." Switzer squinted, then turned to his receptionist and asked her to join them. The young petite blonde shuffled over, wringing her hands, clearly fearing the worst.

"Bonnie, can you tell me if something was here?" Switzer asked her as he pointed at the empty section.

"I can't tell you what that picture was of or who was in it, but I'm sure there used to be one there." She looked at us earnestly, wringing her hands even more feverishly, before adding, "That girl, Victoria, was looking at them right before she left, though I can't say if she took anything with her."

Abe, Elijah and Anna quickly looked at one another. It wasn't much, but it was something.

Anna gently touched the girl on the shoulder. "Hi Bonnie, I'm Anna. We appreciate your help and your honesty. I was wondering, do you happen to know who shot the photographs for the party?" Relief filled the girl's eyes as she realized she wasn't in trouble.

Bonnie nodded. "Well, we all did. It's the same way we do it at all the parties, Mr. Switzer. There are tables with disposable cameras everywhere so anybody can take pictures any time they want."

"Are there negative of these pictures somewhere, Bonnie?" Switzer asked.

"Negatives, sir?" She blinked. "I don't know about that. I'm pretty sure everything is digital. You know, like on a CD?"

Bonnie wasn't trying to offend her boss, she was way too sweet to be rude like that, and young. Abe and Elijah tried to keep from grinning while Anna elbowed them both in the ribs, mouthing for them to stop.

"Um, Bonnie, how many of these cameras would you estimate there were at the party?" Abe asked.

"Five hundred," she replied promptly, "with twenty-seven pictures each. I know because I'm the one who ordered them."

"Wow, that's over 13,000 photos, assuming they all turned out and all the cameras were used." Elijah whistled.

"I currently have all the images on my desktop. I could copy them onto a thumb drive if that would be helpful?" Bonnie offered politely. "Of course, only if it's ok with you, Mr. Switzer?"

"Yes, Bonnie, that would be more than ok. It would be helpful, wouldn't it?" he asked as he turned to the others.

"Absolutely, thank you, Bonnie," Anna replied.

"It will take me awhile, but if you want to grab some late lunch or something, I should have them ready by the time you get back," Bonnie added thoughtfully.

"That's a great idea—best one I've heard all day," Elijah agreed, as his stomach growled loudly.

They asked Switzer if he wanted to join them but the dealership manager graciously waved them off, citing issues that needed his attention. They headed to a nearby chain restaurant, but elected not to discuss the events of the day.

"We've got the whole ride home for that," Abe commented. "No sense giving ourselves indigestion." Anna and Elijah nodded in the affirmative.

As promised, Bonnie had a thumb drive waiting for them upon their return. Before heading back to L.A., they popped their heads into Switzer's office to thank him and say their goodbyes. They also had one final question, something that occurred to them on their way back to the dealership.

"You don't happen to have a picture of Dolby do you?" Abe asked him.

"You know, the police asked me that too. Unfortunately, I don't. Or at least nothing useful. We took a copy of his driver's license when we hired him, but the picture is so grainy, it could be anyone, including my mother-in-law."

"Gotcha, just thought we'd ask," Elijah said. "Thanks for everything, Paul."

"You betcha. I'd love it if you guys would keep in touch and let me know how this thing works out. Of course, if you're ever in the market for a Jag, or want to trade in that tank"—he thumbed at Anna's SUV—"for something classy."

"Gee, Paul, you really know the way to a girl's heart," Anna replied sarcastically.

Always the salesman, Switzer winked and blew her a kiss.

CHAPTER SIXTEEN

It was the following afternoon before I heard back from Sir Edward. He apologized profusely, indicating he had inadvertently let the battery in his cell phone die and hadn't noticed it until that morning.

Heck, I could hardly be upset with him—who hadn't done that? That was until he made a follow-up comment about firing the assistant who had failed to keep his phone fully charged. At my pregnant pause, he burst into laughter.

"I seem to have pulled one over on you, Ms. Jackson," he chortled in a heavy English accent. "I'm sorry. Sometimes I can be quite a naughty old devil."

I laughed lightly. "So your cell phone-charging assistant's job is safe for another day?"

"It'll have to be. Otherwise, I'd be firing myself every other day. I have no assistant to manage my cell or for any other task or any family, for that matter, now the Victoria is gone," he remarked somberly.

"I'm sorry, but losing Joseph and Susan was devastating enough. When I lost Victoria so soon after, it nearly killed me." I heard him gasp. "Oh goodness, please forgive me for my choice of words." A heart-wrenching sob escaped over the connection.

"Sir Edward, I'm the one who should be apologizing. I was so focused on my own agenda it hadn't occurred to me to think about what you must be going through. How you must feel. I'm sorry, please forgive me." It was true. I had forged ahead like a crazed bull, annihilating everything in my path. In doing so, I had exposed feelings he had not yet had time to digest, or heal. I had hurt this man. I felt like a complete and utter jerk.

He only allowed me to wallow in self-pity for a moment. Though sniffling, he quietly said, "No, you don't understand. Receiving your call, hearing your voice…was the most comforting thing I've experienced since Victoria died."

My heart ached as I recognized the voice of loneliness and abandonment. Like me, he had lost his family, his connection to the very thing that binds us to this earth—the thing that grounds us and makes us feel like a part of something—something that has meaning. When I had reached out to him, I had done so for my own selfish reasons, and yet this man had still found in me a kindred spirit. It was at that moment that I realized Sir Edward and I needed one another to gain some semblance of that lost connection.

I put my questions aside for the time-being, and we talked. I told him about growing up in Arizona with my parents, about family vacations, going off to college and my triumphant return home. We talked about my career and laughed over stories of my clients. And, as a dog-lover himself, he was delighted to hear about my adventures with Nicoh.

In turn, he told me about Victoria and her parents and how doting they were, despite their busy schedules. As a child, they took her everywhere they went, immersing her in new cultures and languages and anything else that sparked her interest. He quickly pointed out that while she had grown-up privileged,

Victoria was never spoiled or self-involved. Instead, she was caring and compassionate, taking nothing for granted. She was also fiercely independent. When it came time for her to start thinking about colleges, she refused to allow her parents to influence the admission boards, and was accepted to Columbia University on her own hard work and merit, where she earned a degree in Biomedical Sciences.

Talking about Victoria seemed to lift Sir Edward's spirits, invigorating him. Pride radiated from him as he told story after story. Though they weren't related by blood, he loved her like the daughter he had never had. Their powerful relationship continued from the time she was a toddler, through the awful teen years and as she had entered adulthood. Now reveling in the memories he had collected, he realized he too, had meant the world to her. I felt honored to be able to share that moment with him. Using the back of my hand, I wiped the tears from my cheeks and barely managed to stifle a sniffle before my nose started running. I heard sounds on the other end of the line that led me to believe Sir Edward wasn't faring much better, but neither of us made a comment to that effect.

I had planned on leaving my questions for another call—it certainly didn't seem appropriate to address them now—so I was surprised when Sir Edward asked me to elaborate. I could tell he wasn't simply being polite, so I proceeded.

"I know Jonathan Silverton handled Victoria's adoption for the Winestones. Prior to that, did you know him? Or, did he perform any other services after-the-fact for the Winestones or their company?"

"I had never heard of him until Victoria and I read the contents of the safety deposit box. It did come as somewhat of a surprise because I knew almost all the lawyers they kept on retainer. I used many of them myself, and played a round of two of golf with the rest," he chuckled, before continuing, "but no,

I'm not aware of Joseph or Susan utilizing his services for any other purpose."

"It is so strange," I commented, "his widow didn't mention adoptions being his specialty. If anything, he seems to have been more of a generalist which is curious, because the Winestones had a bevy of lawyers at their disposal. Finding a generalist would have been easy work.

"Besides, Silverton seemed like a random choice for such an important set of circumstances. I didn't know the Winestones—so correct me if am wrong—but from what I've heard about them, it didn't seem as though they would leave something like that to chance."

"You are absolutely correct, they wouldn't have. Having children had always been important to them. If they believed it to be their only opportunity, they wouldn't have subjected themselves to that great of a risk," Sir Edward replied. "There had to have been a valid reason for Silverton's involvement."

"I agree. I wish I could track down Maxwell and Mavis Baumgardner. It seems as though they would be able to shed some light on some of these questions. Perhaps Silverton was their contact, or hired at their suggestion," I mused.

"That's an interesting thought," Sir Edward replied. "Hope this isn't too personal, but you never came across any documents relating to your adoption in your parent's papers, did you?"

"Definitely not too personal," I responded, appreciative of his consideration. "No, not a shred, though I'm not giving up yet. That does bring me to the other question I had for you—is there a possibility the Winestones knew my parents?"

"Arianna, at this point, we can safely assume anything is possible. I can't say I ever recall coming across your parent's names. At least not until Victoria and I found your current birth certificate," he paused for a moment. "Now there's a thought.

What if Silverton was their adoption lawyer, too?" he pondered out loud.

"That would be a very convenient coincidence," I replied. "I've got to see if Leah can track the Baumgardners down. The more we talk about it, the more I believe they are crucial to solving this puzzle."

"Great minds…" Sir Edward started, to which I finished, "think alike."

"They most certainly do, my dear." He chuckled. "I've thoroughly enjoyed, and appreciated our conversation. If I may be so bold to say, I believe I've made a new friend today, though at the same time, I feel like I've known you forever."

"You may indeed be so bold." I laughed. "I too, very much enjoyed and appreciated our conversation, but Sir Edward?" I added, in my best English accent. "If we are to be friends—new or old—you must simply call me AJ."

"Well, turnabout is fair play, my dear. If I must call you AJ, you must call me Sir Harry in return." I was both stunned and touched by his proposition.

"Are you sure?" I managed to stutter. "I thought…only Victoria…"

He cut me off before I could finish. "It's what she would have wanted, AJ. If she was here, she would tell you the same."

I stifled a sob and whispered, "Ok, Sir Harry, but just so you know, you're stuck with me now."

He laughed in a way I knew we'd made a pact. A pinky-swear of sorts.

"AJ, love, I wouldn't have it any other way."

CHAPTER SEVENTEEN

It was late by the time I signed-off with Sir Harry, but I wanted to touch base with Leah and Anna. I knew Leah would still be at the newspaper, so I called her first and filled her in on my activities up to that point—coming up empty in my attempt to locate the Baumgardners and after speaking with Silverton's widow, playing wait-and-see with the information Cheryl Earley said she would collect from the UCMC archive and finally, about generating more questions than answers in my conversation with Sir Harry. Once finished, I had even more mixed feelings about my accomplishments than when I started. For my efforts, had I made any progress?

Surprisingly, Leah reacted more positively than I would have expected. "Wow, you've actually gotten quite a bit of legwork done, Ajax." When I made a noise that indicated I was giving her the scrunchy-face over the phone, she added, "Just because you don't have tangible evidence yet, doesn't mean your efforts were for nothing. It's like that onion analogy, you've got to peel back the layers gradually to see what's underneath. To get to the good stuff. It takes patience, determination, perseverance—" At my groan, she stopped. "What?"

"Isn't this dialogue hijacked from the speech your editor gave at last year's journalism awards party?"

"Not that I remember," she groused.

"Well, I do, because you made me fill in as your date when Boytoy Bobby bailed on you at the last minute. Besides, I think your editor filched it from some macho-high-tech-superhero-spy-action flick."

"Is that even an official genre?" Leah quipped. "Because I'm pretty sure Jason Statham, Vin Diesel and Dwayne Johnson would beg to differ."

"Ok, ok, I'm throwing in the towel on this round. You win. I get what you are saying about the onion. I did some initial work that might not have led us to much yet, but if we keep digging we're bound to find what? A tastier piece of onion?"

"That's the spirit." She giggled. "Now, as your researcher extraordinaire aka BFF, how can I assist?

I gave her a run-down of what I had in mind, taken from the list I had created for her:

Maxwell & Mavis Baumgardner / Sterling Joy Agency

Question: What happened to the Sterling Joy Agency?

Question: What "other opportunities" did the Baumgardners have in mind?

Question: What became of the couple?

Martin Singer / Bio dad

Question: Are there other details surrounding his suicide?

"It's a good start. Just be prepared, the answers will likely lead to more questions," she said when I finished. "In the meantime, what are your plans while you wait for the records from UCMC?"

"I'm going to dig through my parent's papers again, and see if I can find any references to the Winestones or to Silverton, to see if there were any prior relationships there. It's probably too much to expect to find any adoption-specific information among their stuff at this point—I've been through it all a zillion times already—but I'd love to know how the Winestones came into possession of my birth certificates, as well as my parent's address."

"My money is on Silverton or the Baumgardners," Leah said.

"I would tend to agree, but until we track down Silverton's files or the Baumgardners themselves."

"Gotcha—I'll get going on this, but I've got to tell you, you're gonna owe me big time when this is all said and done," she added.

"Let me guess," I replied, thinking of her recent analogy, "onion rings?"

"You got it, girl. Extra crispy with a trough of ranch dressing." Seriously, the girl had a one-track mind.

* * *

My conversation with Anna went a bit more smoothly. Thankfully, no onion analogies were involved. Of course, Anna hadn't put up with me for the better part of her life, either.

I gave her the same rundown of my activities I'd given Leah and afterward, she filled me in on what she, Abe and Elijah had been accomplished.

When she told me about the thumb drive they'd brought back from the dealership, I asked, "Is it possible the missing assistant manager, Tanner Dolby, could be in those photos?"

"That's an interesting thought," Anna admitted. "I could ask Switzer if Dolby worked at the dealership at the time of the

Christmas party. If so, perhaps he would allow Bonnie to look through the photos during her downtime to help us identify him."

"Certainly worth a call. It would be nice to know whether Dolby was involved somehow," I replied. "With everything else that's gone down, it seems unlikely he was in it only to steal a high-priced luxury car."

"I like the way your mind works," she replied appreciatively. "Not to change the subject, but you mentioned some items regarding Silverton you wanted to track down?"

"Yeah, after talking with Sir Harry, we both agreed Silverton was an odd choice for handling Victoria's adoption. Way too random—and risky—for people like the Winestones. Which made us wonder, who recommended him? The Baumgardners? Was he some sort of package deal? If so, did my parents use him too?

"I'd also like to know if Silverton procured the birth certificates and my parent's address for the Winestones, assuming they were not from the Baumgardners. Anyway, I know I'm throwing a lot of miscellaneous stuff out there."

"No, this is all good. It would be huge if Leah caught a lead on the Baumgardners. In the meantime, we can definitely hit the Silverton angle. I have a positive feeling that sometime soon, one of these threads is going to start unraveling."

"I totally agree. Again, thank you, Anna. Please say hi to Abe and Elijah for me."

"Will do," she replied. "Oh, and AJ? You made quite an impression on Sir Edward, for him to ask you to call him Sir Harry."

Though she couldn't see me, I was blushing deeply. "Um, we did get along fairly well, but I don't know about an impression."

"Oh, AJ," she laughed, "you don't fool me. I wasn't *asking* you if you had made an impression on Sir Edward, I was *telling* you that you had."

"Wh-what?" I stuttered, my face on fire at this point. I was sure she could tell, but before I could ponder that any further, she replied, laughing even harder.

"Who do you think he called after the two of you hung up? He wanted to thank me personally for giving you his number. He told me your conversation both inspired and invigorated him. In fact, he's convinced if anyone is going to figure this whole thing out, it's going to be you. So, go Team AJ!"

I wondered, could severe blushing cause second-degree burns?

CHAPTER EIGHTEEN

I awoke the next morning with a sense of anticipation and purpose. Despite the fact we hadn't gleaned much information up to this point, I was convinced we were on the right track, and once we toppled that first hurdle, there would be no stopping us.

I reflected on the events of the past several weeks as Nicoh and I walked briskly through the neighborhood. I was so deep in thought I failed to see my next-door neighbor, Suzy Kemp, waving as we passed her house. Nicoh, however, was on full alert —Suzy typically had snacks in her pocket—and suddenly stopped short, forcing the lead to strain between us. Suzy chuckled as I gasped in surprise, barely catching myself before I face-planted into her ocotillos.

"I'm so sorry, dear. I didn't mean to alarm you." She patted Nicoh on the head and reached into her treasure trove, better known as the snack pocket, as his tail thwapped wildly on the ground. As usual, he was oblivious to the fact he'd nearly graced me with multiple face-piercings—compliments of the ocotillos— in his lust of the elusive Suzy snack.

"It's ok, Suze, it's not your fault." I glared at Nicoh. "I was distracted, though it also appears we both need training."

Suzy laughed. "You were pretty focused. I called out a few times and flopped my hands about like a crazy chicken, but only Nicoh seemed amused."

It was my turn to laugh. "I'm sure your crazy chicken routine was quite entertaining, but I have a sneaking suspicion it was the never-ending supply of snacks you keep in your pocket that drew his attention."

"Oh, that reminds me, I meant to give you this." She reached into the non-snack pocket of her hoody, pulled out a small white envelope and handed it to me.

"As you might remember, I was out of town visiting my sister for the past several weeks." At my nod, she continued, "I had my mail held at the post office and didn't have time to go down and pick it up until now. Anyway, looks like they inadvertently put this in my box." I briefly looked at the envelope. I didn't recognize the handwriting, and there was no return address, though it had been postmarked in Phoenix a few weeks earlier.

"Thanks, Suze, probably an exclusive offer to refinance, or better yet, I've won an all-expenses-paid trip to the Bahamas."

"Well now, perhaps I should take that back?" Suzy teased.

"Weren't you just out of town?" I teased back.

"Honey, did I fail to mention I was with my sister? I believe I've earned that vacation."

We both laughed as I thanked her and we headed home. A FedEx package was waiting on the front step when we got there. It couldn't be the information from Cheryl Earley at UCMC already, could it? I could barely contain my excitement as I hustled Nicoh into the house and threw everything on the counter. After a deep breath, I ripped the box open and whooped at the top of my lungs. It was from Cheryl.

My hands shook as I read the note she had enclosed, which simply read: *AJ—it was truly a pleasure talking to you earlier this week. Enclosed are the documents we discussed. I hope they help you find what you are looking for. Keep in touch—Cheryl.*

Before delving into the contents, I gave her a quick call, and upon receiving her voicemail, left her my thanks. I then called Leah and shared my good news.

"I'll be over in ten," she squealed.

"Really? Are you sure?"

"Are you kidding? This could be more exciting than a Duran Duran reunion tour." I shuddered. Depending upon whose mouth it was coming out of, an exclamation like that could go either way. Fortunately, Leah had been my best friend since we were six, so it was definitely leaning toward the positive.

As promised, she arrived with two minutes to spare, though I hated thinking how many laws she'd broken along the way, especially considering her office was at least twenty minutes from my house, without traffic. I could only stare as she bustled through the door, two Starbucks in hand. My estimate of roadway violations increased two-fold.

"Where is it?" she blurted out as she plunked a beverage in front of me.

"Holy crap, Leah—are you sure you haven't already had enough caffeine?" I began to feel a bit of remorse for her co-workers.

"Sorry, sorry." She dabbed at the liquid she'd slopped on the counter. "I'm really excited!"

"Hmm, I couldn't tell."

"Aren't you excited?"

"Yeah, though I'm not sure it necessitated defying the laws of motion."

"Well, I do," she huffed, but then laughed. "Let's get this show on the road—no pun intended."

We grabbed the FedEx box and settled on my living room floor. Nicoh thought it was some sort of game, so he situated himself in the middle of the action, which meant across both our laps. Did I mention Nicoh is not a lap dog?

Anyway, working around said canine, we pulled the documents out and reviewed them one-by-one as Leah took notes. There wasn't as much in the box as I would have anticipated coming from an organization like UCMC, but it was still a pretty healthy-sized stack. Enough to take us through the end of the afternoon, anyway.

During that time, we managed to weed through enough standardized hospital forms to uphold my conviction of a child-free existence. If Leah had been on the fence about wanting children, she wasn't by the time we managed to make it halfway through the stack. It wasn't all for nothing, however.

We located the requisite medical insurance forms, which contained employment information that would be useful. Martin Avery Singer, MD/Ph.D., was a Geneticist, employed by GenTech. Alison Marie Anders was employed as a Research Assistant of Developmental Biology, Gene Expression and Histopathology at Alcore Ltd.

Crazy titles aside, one thing was for sure, I found it hard to believe two extremely left-brained individuals—scientists, to boot —managed to produce a severely right-brained photographer. I mean, seriously? If I remembered correctly, Victoria's undergraduate degree from Columbia had been in Biomedical Sciences, so one out of two wasn't bad.

Leah immediately noticed the same thing and commented, "Gosh, if it wasn't for you, they would have had the ideal gene pool."

"Sensitive, Leah, real sensitive," I replied sarcastically.

"Sorry, that was bad." In all honesty, her words hadn't offended me. I simply had to take the opportunity to yank her chain when the occasion presented itself.

"There's the soap, should you feel so inclined." I pointed to the pump container on the counter.

"Perhaps I should pace myself," she retorted. "In the meantime, should I add GenTech and Alcore to my research, to find out what they do and what, specifically, your bios did for them?"

"Bios?" I asked.

"Yeah, I figured we could come up with a shortened version of biological parents—a sort of code—to reference them," she replied.

"Ahh, gotcha. Bios works for me, but are you sure you haven't already got enough on your plate? I mean, we haven't even breached this pile yet." I gestured to the plethora of documents in front of us.

"No worries, it might actually help me in researching Martin's suicide. Might give me another angle, too."

We moved on to the medical history forms, which, for our current exercise, contained nothing of merit. Next was the mass of legal documents—living will, things of that nature—you could literally hear the trees crying.

I was glazing over when Leah commented, "I don't understand most of this mumbo-jumbo, but have you noticed what all these documents have told us so far?"

"Do tell," I responded, eager for even a remote break.

"Even though Martin Singer and Alison Anders claimed one another as beneficiaries, they weren't married, nor did they reside in the same location."

"So they conceived out of wedlock. Big whoopee." I had noticed that too, so my response came out a bit more snarky than I'd meant it to.

"I think it's interesting. Could be something there." She pouted.

I'd hurt her feelings. "No, you are absolutely right. It could tie into the bigger picture. What if they worked for competing companies or something?"

"Exactly." She brightened at the thought.

The legal documentation also included final requests and wills, which is where things got interesting. Martin and Alison had included a legal document that expressed their wishes in the event they both passed. In that document, the Sterling Joy Agency would serve as guardian to any living minor children of the couple upon death.

As we read through it, I asked, "Do you think this is the standard procedure, to give something like this to the hospital?"

"I don't know. Maybe they provided it because neither had family," she replied as she wrote on her notepad. I nodded, and we continued reading through the pages, which from both of our expressions, were above both of our legalese-comprehension levels. The last page was signed by Martin and Alison; the Sterling Joy Agency representative, Mavis Baumgardner; a witness named Sophie Allen and finally, the lawyer, Jonathan Silverton.

We looked at one another for a long moment before Leah broke the silence, "Silverton seems to keep popping up all over the place, doesn't he?"

"You've got that right," I responded. "I hope Anna can track down some more info for us because there was definitely something fishy going on with him ...and the Baumgardners."

"No doubt."

"No doubt, indeed."

We made our way through the rest of the legal documents without finding anything that sparked our interest. Next were Alison's medical records, charts, etc. while she had been admitted, which I allowed Leah to review. Apparently, reading medical records was a skill she'd picked up during her reporting assignments. Uh, yeah. Let's just leave it at that.

According to Leah—who paraphrased the documents—Alison

had arrived at the hospital late on June 18 with contractions and gave birth to twin girls in the wee hours of June 19. As they were several weeks premature, the twins were placed in intensive care, but were doing fine. Though exhausted, Alison was also resting comfortably. Three hours after giving birth, she complained of chest pains. Minutes later, she went into cardiac arrest, but the hospital staff was unable to revive her. Alison was officially declared dead three and a half hours after she had given birth to her daughters. Someone had noted the father was not present when she had expired. A signed death certificate was enclosed, in which the cause of death was listed as heart failure. End of story. Like I said, Leah had been paraphrasing. I was certain she had done so for my benefit.

We looked at the next set of documents, which included the twins' medical charts, progress reports, etc. as they stayed on in the hospital. Pretty much what you'd expect until we reached the release forms. The documents indicated a change of guardianship had occurred during their stay. As per the request of Martin and Alison, the Sterling Joy Agency had taken guardianship of the twins, as both parents were deceased at the time. Enclosed was a second death certificate bearing Martin's name. The official cause of death was listed as suicide by drowning, dated five days prior to the change of guardianship. Martin Singer had taken his life less than two weeks after the birth of his daughters and the death of the mother of his children.

While the situation seemed to become more disturbing and confusing with each document we read, something in particular had been nagging at me.

"When Alison arrived at the hospital, she couldn't have known she would be giving birth prematurely—the contractions had come on quickly, without warning—yet she and Martin had all the adoption documentation ready to go. It's almost like they already knew they wouldn't be alive to care for their children."

Leah shrugged in response, as though there was nothing that would have surprised her.

We continued sifting through the last of the items in the box. At this point, it was mostly notes and follow-up documentation—cover-your-booty type of stuff. One thing that caught my eye was the billing statement. Even with today's prices, you could have bought a house and furnished it with the amount that had been due. However, the most intriguing thing about the bill wasn't the total. It was that Martin's company, GenTech, had paid the balance in full.

When I pointed it out to Leah, the look on her face spoke volumes. Maybe there was something left that could surprise her after all.

CHAPTER NINETEEN

Leah was called back to the office. How she was able to be absent from her job for extended periods of time was beyond me. When I asked, all I got in response was a mumbled "external research." I sighed. Leah was a big girl and could handle herself.

I looked at the little pig pen we'd made in the middle of the living room floor and decided I'd better get the papers cleaned up before Nicoh went tromping across them. He was currently dozing beyond the periphery of the mess. He'd had a hard afternoon—napping—after all. I marveled at how he could manage to sleep so much. Honestly, I was a bit jealous.

As I reorganized, I found the Sterling Joy guardianship documentation, which made me think—not once had I seen a reference to Martin and Alison's request. The one where Victoria and I were to be adopted by separate parties. In fact, we only had the Baumgardner's word for it.

I plopped the repacked FedEx box on the counter, the envelope from Suzy catching my eye. In my excitement over Cheryl's delivery, I'd forgotten all about it. I looked at the handwritten address again, only this time I noticed the sender's error. It was addressed using my name, but the street number was off by one house—no wonder it had erroneously been delivered to Suzy. Perhaps I was getting that trip to the Bahamas after all, I chuckled as I ripped the flap.

The envelope contained a single photo of several unfamiliar faces enjoying themselves at what appeared to be a holiday party. There wasn't anything written on the back, though the photo lab had graciously stamped their proprietary information in multiple places. I laughed, it appeared the envelope had been meant for Suzy all along. Surely these people were her friends or family. I picked up my cell phone to call her when it rang. Leah's exuberant voice filled my ear as I answered.

"You were right," she cheered, nearly bursting my eardrum in the process, "GenTech and Alcore were competitors. Both were into genetic engineering. You know, messing around with genes by introducing new DNA?"

"Uh, yeah, how very Wikipedia of you. Anyway, assuming I understand that, go on," I urged.

"Well, remember how scientists cloned that sheep back in the late 1990s?"

"Vaguely," I replied, seriously hoping this wasn't going to be a science lesson. It hadn't been one of my stronger subjects.

"GenTech and Alcore were involved in genetic mutation long before that—specifically with regards to cloning—only they bypassed Mary's little lamb and went directly to Mary."

"Are you telling me they were able to clone humans nearly thirty years ago? Almost fifteen years before the sheep was cloned?" Now things were getting interesting.

"More like attempting to clone humans, but yes, they definitely preceded the sheep. Anyway, GenTech and Alcore were both privately funded, sometimes by the same benefactors. This created a hugely adversarial relationship between the two companies," Leah explained.

"Whoever led the human cloning race received the bulk of the funds," I added.

"Exactly," she confirmed. "Of course, even back then, cloning was controversial, so they concealed their efforts behind other projects—the ones promoted to the public. Again, the more progress a company made, the greater the assistance they received from the benefactors."

"Where do Martin Singer and Alison Anders play into this?" I asked.

"Martin was one of five scientists on the human cloning project at GenTech and Alison was the lead researcher on the same project at Alcore," she replied.

"Wow, that's a serious conflict of interest—which explains why they couldn't come out as a couple—it was probably outlined in their contracts, in triplicate. Both of them could have been terminated if their respective companies had found out about their relationship."

"Interesting choice of words," Leah mused. "Perhaps they had to give up their first-born children and then they were terminated."

"Oh, my gosh, Leah—do you know what you are suggesting?" I growled at her.

"Calm down, it's not like it hadn't occurred to you."

"True," I bristled, my voice several pitches calmer. "I hadn't said it out loud though—that Martin's and Alison's deaths were related to the adoptions."

"Well, I apologize for being insensitive," she said sincerely, "but now that it's out there, here's the real question—were you and Victoria adopted through Sterling Joy because your bios were both dead? Or, did your bios already have to be dead in order for you to be adopted?

"While I'm on a roll, let me add more food for thought. I also researched Martin's suicide. According to witnesses, he walked off the Skyway Bridge on the morning of July 1 during rush hour." She paused to allow me to reflect on the fact Martin Singer had taken his life by jumping off a bridge.

"Though his body was never recovered, based upon the eyewitness' accounts, the location where he went in and the condition of the water, he was officially declared dead and a death certificate subsequently issued. No note was ever found in his apartment or at the lab."

Leah paused again, before adding, "You know, he could have simply been distraught over Alison's death and overwhelmed by the prospect of raising twins alone. Of course, no one would have known about either because he and Alison had been careful to keep their lives separate."

"Someone knew. GenTech footed Alison's hospital bill," I reminded her.

"Yeah, there's that," she replied.

"So, what happened to the project after Martin's death?" I asked.

"Interestingly, it immediately fizzled, but not only for GenTech. Within a month, Alcore went out of business altogether. They had essentially put too many eggs in one basket. No pun intended. GenTech, on the other hand, elected to put their focus elsewhere, claiming the timing wasn't right for human cloning. They are still in the game today, mostly doing medical research, stuff of that nature, but they are nowhere near the industry giant they once were."

"It's almost as though the opportunity slipped through their fingers thirty years ago," I reflected. "Kind of coincidental, don't you think?"

"I guess it depends. Do you believe in coincidences?"

CHAPTER TWENTY

After talking with Leah, I decided to check in with Abe, Elijah and Anna to see how things were going on their end and at the same time, fill them in on what Leah and I had discovered. I hadn't had a chance to find out how she'd gotten that last bit of research so quickly. Leah likely would have claimed trade secrets, which I could have easily gotten her to divulge with a batch of my white chocolate macadamia nut cookies, but perhaps it was better to let sleeping dogs lie.

Anna put me on speakerphone and I began by telling them the medical records from UCMC had arrived, which elicited raucous cheers.

"Nice work, AJ," Elijah exclaimed.

"Cheryl Earley is the one we should be throwing a parade for," I chuckled at their enthusiasm, "but if you like that, then you'll like what Leah and I found *in* the documents."

I proceeded to tell them everything we'd learned, from the guardianship document to the details of Alison's medical records. From there, I explained how Martin and Alison had worked for competing genetics firms while managing to keep their relationship secret, how both companies were involved in human cloning projects that were privately funded by similar benefactors and how the projects fizzled, and the money dried up after Martin and Alison had died, ultimately, putting one out of business while forcing the other to pursue alternate projects. And finally, how Martin's company footed Alison's entire hospital bill.

"Wow, you got all of that—from medical records?" Abe asked.

"Well, from that and the research Leah managed to scrounge up afterward," I replied.

"Shoot, that girl works fast. Maybe we should offer her a job?" Elijah said, only halfway joking.

"After this, she might need one. I'm not exactly sure how she's getting the info, but her editor is going to catch on sooner or later."

"For the sake of this case, let's hope it's later," Abe added. "But after that, let her know we'd like to talk."

I laughed. "I'm sure she'll appreciate that."

"In the meantime," Anna gracefully shifted gears, "we should fill you in on what we've discovered the past couple of days."

"Absolutely, let's do it," I replied, thoroughly excited to hear what they'd learned. I wished Leah was on the call. She would have loved this. I mentally kicked myself for failing to think of that earlier, but made a note for the next time.

"Actually, your research filled in one of our blanks," Elijah began. "When we dug into Sterling Joy's background, we found they were owned by a genetics firm by the name of GenTech. At the time, it didn't mean much, but when you told us they were Martin Singer's employer, a piece of the puzzle fell into place."

"GenTech owned the Sterling Joy Agency?" I asked as another thought rumbled around in my brain. "Wait…that means GenTech undoubtedly would have already known about Martin and Alison's relationship before Victoria and I were born."

"It certainly appears that way, doesn't it?" Abe agreed, then pressed forward, "We also believe Silverton was Sterling Joy's inside man. We aren't completely sure how the whole thing worked, but he typically served as the lawyer for both sides of the adoption. We think the Baumgardners recommended him and encouraged the adoptive parents to utilize his services as a means of ensuring the adoption went smoothly. If this was the case, the Baumgardners essentially used the adoptive parents' insecurities —knowing they wouldn't risk losing the opportunity to have a child—to successfully cover their own bases."

"What about Silverton's other clients?" I asked, still reeling from what I'd heard.

"Regardless of what the man told his wife, we couldn't find any," Abe responded.

"So, what happened to the Baumgardners?"

"They disappeared into thin air. We haven't found a trace of them since they closed the agency. We think Silverton's files went wherever they did," Elijah said.

"So much for pursuing those other opportunities," I commented. "Speaking of the Baumgardners, the other thing that bothers me is their claim Martin and Alison requested separate adoptions, yet there's nothing in the documentation substantiating it."

"It wouldn't surprise me in the least if the Baumgardners made it up," Elijah responded. "Not to be insensitive, but maybe it was more profitable for them to secure adoptions for two different parties, rather than being saddled with a two-for-one deal?"

"Perhaps," I replied, but something told me whatever the Baumgardner's reasoning, it hadn't been isolated to greed.

"Changing the subject to another, slightly less-illuminating topic," Anna piped up, "we are still working our way through the

Christmas party photos from the dealership, trying to identify who or what caused Victoria to bolt.

"After you suggested it, I asked Switzer if the missing assistant manager, Dolby, had worked at the dealership at the time the photos were taken. Switzer confirmed he had and agreed to have Bonnie run through the images on her computer to see if anyone had captured Dolby in any of the holiday shots.

"So far, we haven't found anything useful yet—it's taking a while to get through all 13,000 pictures—but I appreciate your insight."

"Hey, no problem," I replied, "I appreciate you letting me know. I can't imagine having to look through that many photos. Even my own." They all laughed.

"Speaking of photos, you reminded me of one that was delivered to my neighbor by accident. Well, actually, I think it was delivered to me by accident." I proceeded to tell them how Suzy had received an envelope addressed to my name but to her street number.

"When I opened, I found a single photo of a bunch of people I don't know at what looks like a holiday party. There was no return address on the envelope and no notation on the back of the picture other than the proprietary information from the photo lab. Anyway, I think it was actually meant for Suzy." I laughed, noticing the lack of response from the other end of the line.

Anna broke the silence, "AJ, is there a photo number or a jpeg reference next to that proprietary information?"

I knew what she was talking about, but hadn't looked that closely at it the first time. I went to the counter, pulled the photo from the envelope and flipped it over. "Yeah, there's a jpeg reference, it's labeled as IMG 011120.jpg. Does that mean something to you?"

"Maybe," I heard fingers clicking on a keyboard, "describe what you see." I did as she asked, describing everything down to the silly lighted bow ties several of the guys were sporting. Now that I look more closely, I realized the photo was unmistakably of an office party, not a family gathering.

Suddenly, the sound of clicking fingers was replaced by a collective gasp.

CHAPTER TWENTY-ONE

"What is it?" I asked as my heart thudded against my chest.

"We recognize one of the people in this photo," Abe replied, a tremor in his usually-steady voice.

"It can't be. It makes no sense. Why would he…" Elijah's voice trailed off.

"What? What can't be?" I asked nervously.

Ignoring my queries, Abe spoke to either Elijah or Anna, "Let's get Bonnie on the line and have her pull up that photo. Get Switzer involved if you have to."

"What's going on?" I asked again, a little more loudly and forcefully than I had intended. Blame it on the nerves.

"Hang on, AJ, Anna's calling the dealership," Abe replied.

I sat tight and strained to hear Anna as she spoke to Bonnie, but I all I could hear was mumbling. Minutes passed, and I started squirming like a kindergartener anxious for recess.

Finally, the mumbles faded, and Anna's voice came in crystal clear, though there was a hint of shakiness to it, "Both Bonnie and Switzer confirmed it. The person in the photo is Tanner Dolby."

"Unbelievable!" Elijah's voice raged with fury.

Abe's voice matched his brother's, "Bloody hell, there's no

way—no possible way!" I was sure I heard something break on the other end of the connection.

"I…I don't understand," I stuttered, struggling to keep from sounding whiney.

A moment passed before Anna spoke, her voice calmer than either Abe's or Elijah's, but still troubled, "After she saw it, Bonnie was almost positive it was the same photo that had been on the employee bulletin board—the one that went missing after Victoria was there." Tightness began to fill my chest as I waited for her to continue, though I knew where this conversation was heading. "It's the same picture you are holding right now."

"So you think Victoria took the photo from the dealership and then sent it to me after she got to Phoenix?" I thought of the post-mark from a few weeks earlier. The timeframe did fit with her arrival from L.A., but why send it to me? Something else was troubling me.

"This makes no sense. I thought you had never met Tanner Dolby?"

"We hadn't…met him as Dolby," Abe replied, his voice tense. "When we the met the man in the photo, he introduced himself to us a Winslow Clark." The name sounded familiar, but I had read so many documents the past several days that when my mind panned through its index, it came back with a big fat goose egg.

"Clark handled the investigation of your parent's plane crash," Elijah reminded me after my extended silence.

I quietly considered what he was saying: the crash investi-gator and the missing dealership manager were the same person. The other shoe had dropped.

"Tanner Dolby *was* Winslow Clark." Though my voice was barely a whisper, I was sure they heard me, loud and clear.

CHAPTER TWENTY-TWO

"It appears that way, otherwise Dolby was Clark's twin. And frankly, that would be too much of a coincidence," Abe replied. I winced at the thought. Way too much of a coincidence.

I looked at the photo in my hands, at the faces smiling back at me. "Which one is he?" I asked.

"Third from the right," Elijah offered tersely.

Winslow Clark/Tanner Dolby was surprisingly attractive—a pretty-boy type you'd expect to see in a Calvin Klein ad—with artfully-tousled surfer hair and deep-blue eyes that crinkled ever-so-slightly at the corners when he smiled. His teeth were brilliantly white—of the toothpaste commercial variety—which annoyingly, only enhanced his chiseled good looks. I pegged him for my age, but he could have easily gone five years either way. The only flaw in his appearance was the noticeably burnt-out lights on that ridiculous bow tie, and even they curiously added to his magnetism. For as attractive as he might have been, however, Clark/Dolby—or whatever his name currently was—gave me the willies.

"You all knew Victoria, do you find it interesting she would have inadvertently gotten my address wrong on something she believed to be so important?" I asked, after shaking off the unsettling, icky vibe I got from looking at the photo.

Anna replied without hesitation, "Knowing Victoria, she probably intentionally sent the photo to your neighbor, to make sure you got it."

"Especially if she felt she was being followed, or was in danger," Abe added.

"Or was concerned that AJ might be," Elijah thought aloud.

"But why," I asked, "why this picture?"

"It's the one thing that links Clark...Dolby to both the Winestones and your parents," Abe explained. "It's too much of a coincidence that the same person—posing in two entirely different roles—could have been associated with the Winestone's car crash and your parent's plane crash. This was Victoria's proof he was not only tied to both but was involved as well."

I thought for a moment. "Ok, I see where you are going with this, but the Winestones knew Dolby from the dealership, whereas Clark was an investigator on my parent's plane crash after-the-fact. He never actually met my parents," I pointed out.

"True. But who else could do a better job of covering up their handiwork than the person investigating the scene?" Elijah countered. "If he's even a real investigator."

"You're thinking what? That he was in the perfect position to monkey with my parent's plane and the Winestone's car? Without leaving a trace of evidence?" I asked incredulously, though the longer it rattled around in my brain, the more it made sense.

"At this point, anything is possible," Elijah replied. I heard a muffled agreement from Abe, but nothing from Anna.

Something occurred to me. "Wait—didn't you guys talk to Clark? To see if Victoria had followed up with him."

"Yeah, he said he hadn't heard from her since the three of us had met with him," Elijah said.

Abruptly, Anna came on the line. "Well, that confirms it.

While you three were talking, I popped into the other office and tried Clark's number. It's been disconnected."

I froze, "What would you have done if he had answered?"

"Don't worry, I was fully prepared to play the bar floozy and give him a sad little but-I-don't-understand-he-gave-me-this-number song and dance," she chuckled lightly. "Plus, the phone I used is blocked."

"Our girl Anna, both brains and beauty," Abe teased.

"Obviously," she replied sarcastically.

Though I typically would have appreciated their repartee, my head was swimming. Whoever had killed Victoria had done so viciously, publicly and without a hint of remorse. Had Clark/Dolby left a trail of bodies—masked as accidents, deaths by natural cause or suicide, or as people who had appeared to have fallen off the grid? Considering that, I made a mental inventory of possible victims—no matter how far-fetched—that included my parents, the pilot of my parent's plane, Victoria's parents, Jonathan Silverton and of course, Victoria.

If Clark/Dolby was a cold-blooded killer, one thing became apparent as I contemplated my list. If you followed his sick progression, a name was conspicuously missing. Mine. I may not have figured out his end game, but I had a bad feeling about his next move.

Once again, I stared at the photo. Could that enigmatic smile belong to a sadistic killer? I blanched—people had asked the same thing about Ted Bundy.

CHAPTER TWENTY-THREE

Abe, Anna, Elijah and I decided to take a breather and regroup in the morning. In the meantime, I needed to get some fresh air. Perhaps I was naive. I'd seen his handiwork firsthand when I'd found Victoria and should have been scared out of my gourd. Clark/Dolby—if he truly was the killer—wouldn't have hesitated to kill me on the spot. Instead, I was fuming and felt an overwhelming need to vent. So after coaxing Leah into taking a dinner break, I packed a sleepy Nicoh into the Mini and headed to her office.

Silly me, with all my bravado, I failed to check my surroundings as I pulled onto Camelback Road. Had I elected to do so, I would have noticed the white Toyota Camry matching me, turn for turn. We all know what they say about hindsight.

Twenty minutes later, I secured a spot in the parking structure next to the building where Leah's newspaper office was located. As I got out, I was careful to note the level number and section color of the spot I had selected—can you say directionally-challenged? Since we were only three levels up, I opted for the stairs, which didn't win me any points with Nicoh. Finally, we emerged onto the street.

I couldn't take Nicoh into the building, so we waited for Leah in the building's outdoor courtyard and marveled at the skyscraper of glass before us. It should have been peaceful—with the manicured landscaping, beautiful sculptures and luxurious seating—but I was so antsy I could barely sit still. Uncharacteristically, I snapped at Nicoh when he started to sniff some nearby bougainvilleas that bordered the courtyard. His feelings were hurt, so he sat with his back to me, refusing to acknowledge my presence. Great—nothing like a passive-aggressive canine—he'd make me pay for it later.

Leah had warned me she wouldn't be down for a bit, so I took the opportunity to contact Jim Pearce, my parent's former lawyer and friend. I knew he worked late and though I didn't anticipate obtaining anything substantial from him, I needed to keep busy. As expected, he was still in the office and answered on the first ring.

"Hi Jim, it's AJ."

"AJ, how are you doing? It's been awhile—is everything ok? Is there an issue with the house?" Fatherly concern filled his voice.

"No, no, nothing like that. Everything is fine with the house. However, there's something else I wanted to talk to you about. Do you have a minute?"

"Of course, honey, what's going on?"

"Well, this is probably a conversation that is better suited in person, but I'm meeting Leah in a few minutes and well, time is of the essence."

"I understand. Just tell me, what is it?"

"Well, um, there's no easy way to say this, but I recently found out I was adopted," I said bluntly.

"I see," his tone indicated he had known, but I needed further confirmation.

"Did you know?" I asked gently. "I'm not trying to put you on the spot here, Jim. I'm looking for some specifics about the adoption and hope you can help.

I heard a deep sigh on the other end before he responded, "I did, but after-the-fact." He then told me a story that sounded eerily similar to the one Sir Harry had told about a busy, working couple who found out too late in life they couldn't have children, so they decided to adopt. And, like the Winestones, my parents were very private about the details, but one day, there I was. He hadn't been involved in the adoption, nor did my parents speak of it until several years later.

"Your father only briefly mentioned the adoption once, and at the time, he was strangely agitated. The lawyer he and your mother had used for the adoption—someone the agency had highly recommended—had sent him some documents related to the adoption he found troubling. Just sent them out-of-the-blue. Nearly thirty years later. He hadn't told your mother about the documents, for fear they would upset her, but realized he would need to come clean with both of you at some point. I never got the opportunity to bring it up again. They died in the plane crash a week later."

He paused briefly, but I remained silent, allowing his words to register. "After they were gone, I wasn't sure it was my place to tell you. I didn't want to cast a shadow over your memories of them. I'm so, so sorry, AJ."

"Jim, I understand. And I don't blame you. My parents had their reasons. I…I'm sure they were doing what they thought was best at the time. I loved…love…them unconditionally. Nothing will ever change that." I fought back a sob as a single tear escaped down my cheek.

"Thank you for understanding, AJ," Jim sighed.

"Thank you, Jim, for your honesty," I replied sincerely. "Out of curiosity, did my father happen to mention the name of the adoption lawyer?"

"Hmm, if memory serves, it was Silver-something," Jim recalled.

"Silverton?" I asked hopefully.

"Yes, that's it. Silverton," he confirmed.

Bingo. Another piece of the puzzle slid into place.

I saw Leah coming out of the front entrance, so I thanked Jim, told him we would meet for lunch soon and said my goodbyes.

"Hey, what's up?" Leah plopped down on the chair next to mine and scruffed Nicoh's ears before slipping him a cookie.

"Besides the fact you are turning my dog into a chunky monkey?" I sniped as I gave her the evil eye, which as usual, she waved off. I decided to tell her about my call to Jim before proceeding on to the details of my conversation with Abe, Elijah and Anna. The way she had scrunched up her face and plucked at the spiky wisps jutting from her head told me she was miffed about not receiving an invite to the latter.

"I know that look, Leah. You've already helped me immensely. Plus, you can't keep ducking out of work."

"Don't worry about it. I've got it under control. My work is getting done, despite my extracurricular activities. Next time, I want in. Or else." Based upon previous experience, such veiled threats usually resulted in adding an extra five pounds to my dog's already enormous physique.

Adequately chastised, I told her about GenTech's ownership of the Sterling Joy Agency, which garnered me an intrigued "oooooh," how Silverton was servicing both sides of the adoption —as Jim had confirmed was the case in my adoption—and finally, of the Clark/Dolby connection. Leah was as floored as the rest of us had been, then horrified when I added in my theory about his list of victims.

"Oh my, AJ, if you are right, do you think that sicko left Victoria's mutilated body for you to find on purpose? You know, a way of putting you on notice?"

I shuddered. "I have no idea. I mean, maybe I'm getting us both worked up by drawing conclusions where there are none. What if Victoria's murder was an isolated incident?"

"Come on, AJ," Leah threw her hands up as she launched off her seat, "do you really believe that?"

I didn't, but the alternative was terrifying. "No. I don't. However, whether Clark/Dolby is our guy, we're missing a key piece of the puzzle."

"Explain." She had calmed down significantly but still stood rigidly, hands on hips, facing me.

"If you look at all the breadcrumbs we've collected so far, from the accidents, to the people that have gone MIA, to Victoria's murder," I paused to look at her earnestly, "all roads eventually lead us back to Alcore and GenTech."

"Six-degrees of separation," she murmured.

I absently nodded. "We've got to go back to the beginning. Find people who either knew about or were involved in the feud between Alcore and GenTech. People who worked with either Martin or Alison."

"Easier said than done," Leah said as she began tormenting her hair again.

"Even for a hotshot reporter like yourself?" I teased.

"As if." She pretended to pout. "I've got connections."

"Top-secret   you'd-have-to-kill-me-if-you-told-me-type connections?

"You know it. Give me until morning?" I stood as she turned to head back up to her office.

"Absolutely. And Leah?"

"Yeah?" she paused, looking at me.

"Thanks for everything." I moved forward and gave her a quick hug.

She hugged me back, even tighter. "Anytime, Ajax, anytime."

Even with the courtyard lights on, it was still dark, so I

watched until I saw her head bob into the building, then nudged Nicoh with my foot.

"You ready to go, buddy?"

He grumbled in response and took his time stretching as he got up, pausing to sniff the bougainvilleas I had scolded him about earlier. This time, I pretended not to notice and instead took a moment to survey my surroundings. The lights must have been playing tricks on me. For a moment, I thought I saw something in the shadows off to the side of the building, but when I squinted, it was gone. I shivered, then chuckled to myself. I needed to get a grip. The past few weeks were messing with my head.

We made our way back to the parking structure and up the three flights of stairs to our level, now less than halfway full, because of the hour. I reached into my bag to pull out my keys, and once again thought I sensed movement in the shadows. Rather than appease my curiosity, I listened to hairs on the back of my neck and hustled Nicoh to the vehicle. Once we were safely locked-in, strapped-in and the vehicle was revved-up, I quickly peered from side-to-side and front-to-back. Boogeyman-free, I shifted into drive and got the heck out of Dodge.

My senses were still working overtime, so I glanced in my rearview mirror more frequently than I normally would have, which is how I spotted him. He exited the parking structure in a white Toyota approximately twenty seconds after I had. At first, I just figured it was paranoia and took an alternate route home to prove it to myself, opting to weave through a myriad of neighbor-hoods instead of traveling the main streets. My heart dropped. At every turn, he was there, lurking 200-300 feet behind. I'd watched enough Burn Notice episodes to realize this was not a loose tail, especially after my seventh right-hand turn.

Thoroughly freaked-out, I did the only thing I could think of at that moment. I called Ramirez.

CHAPTER TWENTY-FOUR

Ramirez wasn't on duty when I called, but fortunately, he was nearby and directed me to his location. Of all places, he was at Starbucks. At night. Guy must need to get his coffee buzz on at all hours. I mentally slapped myself—who was I to judge? Right now, I was in dire need of his assistance and thanks to his late-night caffeine therapy session, he was able to come to my aid. A shout out to baristas working late everywhere.

As I pulled into the parking lot and eased into the first available space, the Toyota passed. Though the driver didn't look in my direction, I caught a glimpse of something familiar. An Arizona Diamondbacks hat. I know, you're probably thinking, duh, you're in Phoenix—it'd be pretty common to see people wearing the home team's swag—and you'd be right.

This hat was distinctive, though, a piece of memorabilia from the 1998 inaugural season. At the time, only one hundred bearing the design had been made. I knew this because Leah's dad, a well-known sportscaster at the time, helped me procure one for my dad's fortieth birthday. On the inside, it had the imprint: #40 of 100. Leah's dad had Andy Benes, a pitcher at the time, sign the bill of the hat, along with owner Jerry Colangelo and manager Buck

Showalter. It was my dad's favorite hat. So much so, he wore it all through my high school and college years. He was wearing it the last time I hugged him goodbye—as he and my mother rushed out the door to catch their flight to Albuquerque, where they would catch another small commuter flight to Colorado Springs. Within twenty-four hours, they would both be gone.

I hadn't seen a hat like it since. That was until I'd met with Abe and Elijah a few days earlier. At this very Starbucks, in fact. The man sitting alone at the table behind us had been wearing a similar hat, though I hadn't thought about it much at the time. We'd been having a pretty heavy conversation, and I had been glad to escape it for a few minutes while Nicoh did his business. Had the man been eavesdropping? Could it have been Clark/Dolby? I thought back to the photo of the man known as Dolby and shook my head. I hadn't been able to see much with the way he had positioned himself at the table, his hat pulled low. However, now that I'd seen a similar man and hat in the span of a few days, I was taking nothing to chance. I jumped when Ramirez lightly tapped on the window.

"Sorry," he murmured when I opened the door to get out, "I didn't mean to startle you. Are you ok?"

"No, it's not your fault, I was distracted. And yeah, I'm ok now, thanks. Just a bit of a disconcerting ride over. Did you see him?" I glanced toward the street, but the Toyota was long gone.

"I did." He looked at me carefully, as though I was going to crack right before his eyes. Wow, did I look that frazzled? *Note to self:* Immediately consult mirror after indulging in Mr. Toad's Wild Ride, especially when a hunky guy is involved.

"California plates—was able to get a number. I'm not expecting much, but I'll run it through the system, see what pops up."

"Good. Thanks. You have a minute? I'd better fill you in on a few things." When Ramirez nodded, I collected Nicoh and the three of us headed to the same patio table where Abe, Elijah, Leah and I had sat. I plopped into the chair, suddenly weary. The adrenaline had worn off, and the day's events were finally catching up with me. I needed to pull it together long enough to get Ramirez up to speed.

I'm not sure what I expected, but when I finished, his steely gaze fixed on me, his lips drawn into a tight, thin line. My eyes popped—was he angry with me?

I opened my mouth to speak, but he put his hand up and quietly uttered, "AJ, I'm sorry. I should have never pushed you into getting involved."

I started to protest and once again, his hand rose to stop me. "You are in over your heads. All of you."

Perhaps I was too tired at this point to control my emotions because his condescending tone made me snap. "Yeah? Well, I may be in over my head, Detective, but please do tell, what have you and your FBI pals come up with so far?" I snarled, sarcastically emphasizing "Detective."

"Darn it AJ," he growled, "you're going to get yourself killed."

"As opposed to getting myself killed waiting around?" I spat, undeterred by his outburst. "A killer is out there and if you think I'm going to sit by and take things as they come, or wait for someone to save the day, you are sorely mistaken."

"You seem to have needed saving this evening, AJ," Ramirez snarked, but once he witnessed the fury burning in my eyes, I knew he regretted the words the minute they'd escaped. Given my mood, I wasn't about to let him off the hook.

"My mistake. One I won't be making again." I tugged on Nicoh's leash, and for once, he didn't dawdle as I hustled him toward the car. After a few steps, I turned on my heel and faced

Ramirez, who stood stoically, hands on hips, an indecipherable expression on his face.

"And just to be clear—your apology is not accepted. If you gave me that information expecting a different result, you severely underestimated the girl you thought me to be," I hissed.

"Furthermore, this may be too much for your ego to absorb, but I don't need anyone coming to my rescue. My nickname is Ajax for a reason. You'd do well to remember that in the future, Detective." I left him standing there as I marched purposefully to the Mini, and after quickly situating Nicoh and myself, sped out of the parking lot.

Had I spared a look back in Ramirez's direction, I would have seen the slightest hint of a smirk playing on his lips.

CHAPTER TWENTY-FIVE

I grumbled as the alarm chirped happily. Morning arrived too soon, following a stress-filled day and sleepless night. Adding to the irritation was the persistent beep echoing from my cell phone, conveniently out of reach across the room on the dresser. I negotiated my way around Nicoh, who had once again monopolized the majority of the bed and was currently running joyously in his uninterrupted sleep. No doubt dreaming of the elusive Pandora. If only my life were that simple.

I sighed as I looked at my phone, then immediately wished I had stayed in bed. Ramirez had left me a message. Great. Maybe he'd gotten a clue and decided to apologize for real this time. Realistically, the odds of that were about as likely as Nicoh sleeping on his own doggie bed. I queued up the voicemail and prepared for the worst.

Ramirez's message was brief, "Got a match on the plate. The Toyota is registered to Tanner Adam Dolby of Santa Monica, California. Do with it what you will, AJ." Ignoring the curt delivery, I focused on the message itself.

I needed to contact Abe and Elijah ASAP, but before I could finish that thought, my phone rang to the sound of Leah's ringtone, Duran Duran's *Notorious*. As soon as I answered, she blurted, "Wait 'til you hear what I've got for you!" At my silence, her excitement dimmed. "What's wrong?"

I told her about my mad dash through the streets of Phoenix, meeting with Ramirez at Starbucks—including a play-by-play of our tiff—and his follow-up call this morning.

"So we have confirmation Dolby is in town, stalking you, waiting for the perfect moment to swoop in and—"

"Stop," I gritted out through clenched teeth, "this is my life, not one of your stupid articles."

"Whoa—someone got up on the wrong side of the bed. Don't you dare snark at me, Arianna Jackson." Immediately, I regretted my snottiness and started to apologize when she added, "Don't forget I know what you looked like before you had braces and have the pictures to prove it." After a moment, we both burst out laughing.

"I'm sorry, Leah. I'm being a total jerk."

"Yes, you are, but that's what I'm here for, to de-jerkify you when you need it. You are fortunate I'm always on my best behavior and never in need of such services in return." Again, laughter filled both sides of the connection. "Clark/Dolby-related issues aside, do you want to hear why I called?"

"Absolutely," I replied.

"I have a friend at the *Chicago Tribune* who owes me a favor," she began.

"Wait, what friend?" I asked, suddenly suspicious and dreading her response.

"Michael Rafferty," she briskly replied. I groaned. Michael had been Leah's college boyfriend. They had dated for a year until he moved on to greener pastures, meaning the busty editor of the school paper. In an attempt to mend Leah's broken heart, we had both gained five pounds indulging in chocolate Oreo cookie ice cream. Michael eventually regretted his fling with the editor, who hadn't given him the choice stories he had hoped his association with her would garner, and tried to make amends with Leah. Though she'd repeatedly rebuffed his apologies, he'd pop out of the woodwork every few years in an effort to rekindle the relationship. To date, I thought she had succeeded in warding him off.

"I can hear the gears working in that melon of yours, AJ," she warned. "Just for the record, I'm not giving Rafferty the time of day. He owes me a favor. As a colleague. Which I'm cashing in. For you. So thank me and let's get on with it."

"Thank you, Leah," I replied sincerely. "I do appreciate your assistance."

"As you should," she teased. "Anywhoo, I gave Michael the bare minimum—nothing involving you or Victoria—said I was looking for information on Alcore and GenTech, their ongoing feud, the demise of Alcore, etc. I made it clear I wanted the behind-the-scenes goods, not the stuff edited for public consumption.

"Anyway, Rafferty did one better. He found us someone who had first-hand knowledge, a former bureau chief by the name of Mort Daniels. And this is where it gets good. Turns out, Daniels retired back in the 1990s and moved to sunny Ahwatukee, Arizona."

"No way. I can't believe we'd get that lucky."

"I know. That's not even the best part. Rafferty contacted Daniels and set up a meeting. Daniels wanted time to pull some of his old notes, but he's able to see us in a couple of hours."

"That's awesome. Rafferty must want to get back into your good graces," I remarked.

"Don't you worry, missy." Leah chuckled mischievously. "Like I said, he owes me."

"Whatever, I appreciate it. You want me to swing by and pick you up?" I asked.

"Yeah, see ya in a few," she chirped happily as she hung up.

I looked at the clock. My call to Abe and Elijah would have to wait.

Nicoh and I picked Leah up at her condo forty-five minutes later and headed to Daniels' home in the Ahwatukee Foothills. The ride was unusually quiet, as both of us deep in thought. I can't speak for Leah, but I was also more than a little anxious about our impending meeting. Fortunately, before the anxiety manifested into a full-blown panic attack, we arrived at our destination.

Daniels lived in a gated community filled with carefully-maintained custom-built homes. His house was located at the back of a cul-de-sac and was spacious without being pretentious. He greeted us as we pulled into his turnaround driveway, a smiling man of tall stature and slight build. I pegged him for late 60s or early 70s, but there was a twinkle in his eye that led me to believe he was as spry as a man half his age.

After introductions were made, he gestured for us to join him in the backyard for iced tea. We ooo'd and ahh'd at the enchanting landscape. Flowers and plants of various species and colors intermingled artfully along the cobblestone pathway, which lead to an outdoor seating area filled with lush chairs in richly-colored fabrics. A small natural stone waterfall cascaded gently into the koi pond below, producing a soothing background rhythm for the already serene surroundings.

"Lovely," I murmured as Leah nodded, her eyes wide as they roamed over every detail.

"Thank you," Daniels beamed, "it's always nice to hear one's handiwork is appreciated."

"You did all of this?" Leah asked, using both arms to gesture toward the landscape the surrounded us.

"Sure did." He chuckled. "Of course, it was dumb luck. When I moved in, it was nothing but dirt back here. And bugs. Lots of 'em. What was meant to be a quick stop at Home Depot to pick up some insecticide turned into a two-year project," he paused as both of us gawked at him, open-mouthed. "Anyway, long story short, I found something to keep myself busy during retirement."

We all laughed as he motioned for us to sit. He poured tall glasses of iced tea while we made small talk, discussing items such as landscaping in the desert and our black thumbs. Ours, not his. Once we were all situated—even Nicoh had his own water bowl with ice cubes—Daniels got down to business.

"Michael told me you were looking for some background information on Alcore and GenTech from back in the day?" When we both nodded, he continued, "Well, you're in luck. Those two happen to have been pet projects of mine." He pulled a large file box from around the side of his chair and removed the lid. Inside were dozens of folders, neatly arranged by month and year.

"Michael also said you had already done some initial research. Don't hesitate to let me know if I'm rehashing familiar territory." He smiled at us warmly as he absently rubbed Nicoh behind the ears.

"As you are likely aware, Alcore and GenTech were fierce competitors in the field of genetic engineering, often battling for funding from the same sources. Though both companies had other projects, these sources were primarily interested in the human cloning aspect of the science."

"And where the money goes, the project focus goes as well," Leah added.

"Exactly," Daniels continued, "and with the money also came protection. Not only was genetic mutation controversial, even the mere thought of human replication moved the science into an entirely different arena. One with moral and ethical consequences. Alcore's and GenTech's benefactors carried the clout to shelter them from the pandemonium that would have ensued had government and religious sectors got involved."

"What was going on at Alcore and GenTech?" I asked, hoping

I hadn't disrupted our host's train of thought. If I had, he didn't let on.

"According to my source—"

"Your source?" Leah inquired, though as a reporter herself, she knew what his response would be.

"To this day, I have not divulged his identity, though I can confirm he had intimate knowledge of the day-to-day operations at GenTech and was familiar with Alcore's as well. For today's purposes, we shall call him X. Please pardon the cliché." He chuckled.

"Anyway, according to X, both companies were attempting to replicate a human life—a child—by isolating non-reproductive cells from the mother. Once they had removed these donor cells, their nuclei would be transferred to a host cell. Though the scientist's methods were radically different at each company, the host cell in each scenario was chemically altered to the point it behaved like one generated during the union of female egg and a male sperm. The resulting host cell contained all the DNA necessary to develop into a human child. Once the host cell evolved into an embryo, it was implanted back into the mother and carried to a full term.

"In natural reproduction, half of a child's DNA comes from the mother and the other half from the father. With cloning, the DNA comes entirely from one source: the mother. The resulting child is a genetic replica of that source."

"Wow—that could make for an interesting family dinner, say if a mother gives birth to a daughter," I thought aloud.

"Ugh, can you say daddy issues?" Leah added. "And what about the mother-daughter relationship—could you imagine getting into an argument with yourself?"

Daniels watched us, obviously amused by our banter, but when he spoke again, his tone was serious. "And therein lies some of the ethical concerns with regards to human cloning." We both nodded in agreement, though we could certainly think of others.

"So, how many mothers were involved in the experiment?" I asked, moving the conversation away from the unsettling ethical dilemmas the subject brought to mind.

"GenTech had six mothers come to full term, and while Alcore had twice as many volunteers in their program, none of them made it through the entire gestation period."

"After all of that, there were only six offspring?" Leah asked, a perplexed expression crossing her face.

Daniels sighed, scratching his head. "Well, that's where things got a little fuzzy. A little grayer, perhaps. Each mother was actually implanted with two embryos. X said GenTech wanted to pad the odds, to ensure at least one made it to term. That was one of the reasons, anyway."

"Meaning if they did come to term, the mother would have had twins?" I asked.

Daniels nodded. "It's sketchy whether all came to term—even X wasn't sure—but yes, had they all survived, there would have been twelve children. Six sets of twins. All girls." We all took a moment to reflect on that tidbit.

Leah broke the awkward silence. "You said 'one of the reasons' GenTech implanted two embryos—what was another?"

His friendly demeanor immediately turned to one filled with disgust and distaste. "There were rumors—that not even X could fully substantiate—GenTech was also creating the twin as a means of providing 'spare parts,' for lack of better phrasing."

"Oh my," I whispered as I looked to Leah, her eyes wide and mouth opened in shock.

"There were other rumors, too, that painted darker pictures of their intentions." Daniels shook his head, sickened. "I can't even begin to bring myself to utter the words."

"Don't," Leah said gently. "What I don't understand is how

the mothers would knowingly subject themselves or their unborn children to that possibility?"

"They didn't know," Daniels replied. "I'm not sure about Alcore, but prior to the cell extraction, GenTech required the mothers to sign an agreement relinquishing all rights to any child born as a result of their participation in the program. They used the awkward family dynamic you mentioned as their BS rationale. Of course, after considering the alternatives, the mothers quickly acquiesced. Plus, they were handsomely rewarded for their cooperation.

"But GenTech didn't stop there when it came to getting the mother's consent. They also guaranteed the children would be adopted separately, to parents in different states. This limited the possibility the mother or any of her other non-program children would come into contact with the cloned child during their lifetimes. That time clock started the moment she gave birth."

Something clicked into place as Daniels spoke, but I wasn't sure exactly what.

"How come you never ran the story?" Leah asked, changing the subject.

"By the time I was able to collect all of this," he motioned toward the file box, "the benefactors had lost their footing—too many hands in the pot—and the Feds, as well other public and private sectors were rapidly closing in. As a result, their purse strings tightened, forcing GenTech to return their focus to the other—pre-cloning—projects and Alcore to close altogether.

"Despite the shift, I continued tracking GenTech, but many of those involved in the project were quickly transitioned out. Others couldn't or wouldn't talk, or they conveniently disappeared. No one wanted that cat coming out of the bag, so keeping it quiet from that point forward wasn't an issue."

"Unless you were a newspaperman," Leah added.

Daniels' head bobbed in agreement. "Unless you were a news-paperman."

"So, out of curiosity, did the cloning program ever have a name?" I asked.

He nodded, chuckling. "I could never decide if the GenTech scientists who named it did so out of total madness or pure genius. Anyway, in the early days of the project, they simply referred to it as Gemini."

The astrological sign of the twins.

With all that I had heard today, my money was on the prior —madness.

CHAPTER TWENTY-SIX

Daniels looked at us intently, as if making a decision about something important. Finally, he spoke, "I'm hoping you will entertain a question in return?" At our nods he continued, "After all these years, why are you really interested in Alcore and GenTech?" I looked at Leah, and she bobbed her head in the affirmative—we could trust Daniels with the truth.

"My interest lies with Martin Singer, a former scientist at GenTech and Alison Anders, a researcher at Alcore. I recently learned they were my birth parents," I paused before Leah and I proceeded to give him the *Reader's Digest* version of the past several weeks. When we were finished, he was unnervingly quiet for a long while.

"Interesting. That definitely changes things." He reached forward and dug through his file box, extracting a single photo. "I thought you looked oddly familiar."

He handed me an 8" x 10" photo of a group of roughly thirty men and women in stark white lab coats—the only splash of color provided by the orange and blue Alcore logo on the left breast pocket. Several individuals had crossed arms, with serious faces. This certainly wasn't one of your school photos where someone makes a ridiculous face or forms rabbit ears with their fingers behind the teacher's head. These people looked annoyed, as if posing for the photo had been an unnecessary distraction in their busy day—an impediment to the progression of their important work.

"This was the team involved in Alcore's cloning project," Daniels offered, pointing to a single face in the group.

Leah and I squinted at the woman he had indicated. "Whoa, that's creepy," Leah whispered as I sucked in a shallow breath. A mirror image of my own face stared back.

My birth mother, Alison Anders.

"I see the resemblance, but you recognized me from this?" I gestured toward the one-inch orb that was Alison's face. Daniels laughed heartily, a deep rumbling sound.

"No dear, I had the honor of seeing her in person, plus the benefit of a photographic memory." He tapped his temple. "I've got pictures from GenTech too, of Martin Singer, but you certainly favor your mother. I assume your sister did too?"

I shuddered as I thought of the last time—the only time—I had ever seen Victoria in the flesh. I didn't want to remember her that way, yet the vision was forever embedded in my memory. I forced it down, and thought back to the photos Ramirez had brought me of her twinkling eyes and smiling face. Finally, I nodded at Daniels.

"I'm so sorry, dear, I didn't mean to—" I put a hand up to stop him.

"It's ok. I'm trying to get my head around all of this." I chuckled lightly, sadly. "Half the time I don't know what to think or feel." Leah rubbed my shoulder as Daniels looked at me, his eyes filled with compassion.

"I was sorry to hear Martin and Alison had passed. I doubt anyone knew they were involved with one another. X certainly didn't mention it," he added, thoughtfully.

"Given the sensitivity of the projects they were working on, not to mention the ongoing hostility between their companies, I'm sure they would have both been terminated had their affair come to light. Besides, it would have been a violation of both of their employment contracts.

"No, I'm quite sure no one was wise to their liaison. And, the proximity of their deaths didn't set off any alarms either. There was too much else going on at the time," he paused, remembering the past.

"Earlier, you said 'that definitely changes things'—what did you mean?" Leah asked.

"Please, don't get me wrong. When we were talking before, I wasn't leaving things out to purposely deceive you, I didn't think they were relevant to your research at the time. Now that I know the whole story, they may be pertinent.

"When the benefactors pulled their money, forcing the cloning projects to be terminated, and Alcore to close, it was rumored Martin Singer had gone into the GenTech lab and removed all the formulas and procedures required to develop the clones so they couldn't be reproduced—or misused—in the future.

"The same week, after Alcore had let everyone go, their cloning lab suddenly went up in flames. It was blamed on faulty wiring, but interestingly enough, it was the only area in the entire building that sustained any damage."

"Surely no one thought Martin had orchestrated that little mishap, too?" I queried.

"Nothing could be substantiated, but X said there was specu-lation. Now that I know of the connection between Martin and Alison though—" Leah abruptly cut Daniels off, surprising the older man.

"Come on—you are not seriously considering the notion Alison provided Martin with the means to sneak into enemy terri-tory, undetected, so he could destroy the lab?" I tended to agree with her, the idea seemed rather outlandish. "Let's not forget she died before the projects ended and Alcore closed."

Quickly overcoming his surprise at Leah's outburst, Daniels chuckled. "Just thinking out loud, my dear, forgive an old, rambling mind."

I spared a look to Leah, neither of us was buying it. After divulging all that he had, why hold back now?

"So, after Martin committed suicide, the formulas were never found?"

"No, to this day, the formulas and procedures have never been found. Whatever secrets he held went with him. When he died, effectively, so did the project," Daniels added, his face unreadable.

"Convenient, don't you think?" Leah commented.

Convenient, I silently agreed, but for who?

"Then why is there a killer still out there?" I asked of no one, in particular.

It was Daniels who replied, "Now that's the million-dollar question, isn't it?"

CHAPTER TWENTY-SEVEN

Daniels waved goodbye to the girls as they pulled out of his driveway. Once they were safely out of sight, he pulled a disposable cell phone from his trousers and dialed the number he'd only used on two other occasions, nearly thirty years earlier.

After all that time, the same crisp voice answered on the third ring. Always on the third ring.

"How much did they know?" the voice inquired, emphasizing each word in an almost painful, unyielding way.

"Enough," Daniels replied, "they knew enough."

"He won't be pleased," the voice replied, the tone unchanged.

"No, I expect he won't," Daniels said in return.

This time, there was no reply, only a deafening silence on the other end of the connection.

CHAPTER TWENTY-EIGHT

We were on the outskirts of Daniels' neighborhood when Leah turned to me. "Super nice man—kind of lonely in a sweet way—but something was definitely up."

I nodded. "Do you think we should have held off telling him why we really wanted to talk to him?"

"No way. Telling him got us that last little nugget on Martin. And these." She shook the envelope containing photos of the former Alcore and GenTech employees Daniels had lent us. "Besides, he's probably harmless."

She had a point, though I wasn't sure I totally agreed with her on the last one. Honestly, I didn't know why. Chalk it up to a gut thing. I momentarily put it on the back burner, electing to focus instead on our conversation with Daniels.

"Pretty crazy stuff going on at Alcore and GenTech back in the day, huh? Can you believe they were actually replicating humans thirty years ago?"

"I know. Can you imagine what those formulas could have morphed into if scientists had been improving upon them over the years?" She scrunched up her face.

"I know. I wish I could simply look at the benefits associated with that project, but when Daniels mentioned the whole spare parts bit, I nearly barfed." I blanched at the thought. "Certainly makes you stop and think twice, doesn't it?"

"This may be taking it to the extreme, but what if someone had developed an entire army of clones—the perfect soldiers—to serve as the ultimate wartime killing machines? Yeesh, think of what could have happened had those formulas gotten into the wrong hands."

"Sounds like the plot of a campy sci-fi horror flick to me, and fortunately, that was not the case."

"Yeah, thanks to Martin, but what do you think happened to the children who came out of the Gemini project?"

"Hard to say. If they truly were adopted, as Daniels suggested, then we can only hope they are leading happy, normal lives." Leah looked at me, a bit sadly and nodded.

"But his reference to the adoption agreements, you realize what that means, right?"

I nodded, having already considered the idea. "We've got yet another thread to tie the Sterling Joy Agency to GenTech. Though he didn't name them specifically, we already knew GenTech owned them, probably for that very purpose." Ugh. It seemed so all-in-the-family. Double ugh—no pun intended.

"Yeah, I noticed Daniels didn't go into too many details on that particular subject."

"Me too. In thinking over the conversation, he was pretty careful—giving us bits he wanted us to know, leaving others out —but why? What would be his motivation? It wasn't as though you were going to run away with his pet story after all these years and publish it yourself." I snorted. I truly didn't believe that was Daniels' rationale.

We were so deep into our conversation, we arrived at Leah's office before we both knew it. Considering the amount of time we had spent with Daniels, we agreed it would be better if I dropped her off at work and then picked her up later. I watched her as she got out the Mini, collected her things and gave Nicoh a hug and some scratches.

"Thanks, Leah," I said earnestly. "I appreciate you contacting Rafferty. The interview with Daniels was definitely worth it."

"My pleasure, Ajax. I'd do anything for you." She patted the side of the car. "I'll give you a call when I'm ready to take off for the night. In the meantime, have fun perusing the Alcore/GenTech I'm-too-serious-to-be-sexy glamour shots." She giggled and bounded off in the direction of her office building.

I was still laughing when I pulled into my own driveway. That was until I realized I hadn't called Abe and Elijah about Clark/Dolby yet. Crap. Any messages? Nope. Good. I tried their office, and when Anna picked up, she put me on hold while she called Abe's cell, returning momentarily, once she has us all connected.

Elijah called out, "How're things in Phoenix, AJ?"

"Interesting, to say the least," I said, my tone serious as I proceeded to tell them about the tail the previous night, my suspicions it had been Clark/Dolby and finally, Ramirez's confirmation this morning the car was registered to Dolby.

I could hear one, if not both, of the guys start to comment, but I pressed on and told them of the morning Leah and I had spent with Mort Daniels, including our after-commentary and analysis. I wrapped up, letting them know the photos Daniels had given me were next on my agenda. Finally, I expelled a deep breath.

Anna spoke first, "Um, AJ? I think you might have blown someone's gasket. A couple gaskets, actually."

"Wh…what?" I stuttered, but before she could respond, the floodgates opened and two enraged brothers came tumbling out.

For several minutes, they both read me the riot act. I won't go into the back and forth dialogue, but it was certainly colorful and went along the lines of a classic *Dick and Jane* book. The basic plot of this particular story being stupid girl doesn't think, stupid girl acts carelessly, stupid girl gets into trouble, stupid girl gets dead. Oh no, poor stupid girl. Redundant and annoying, isn't it?

After the riot act came the directive.

"So, Ms. Jackson," Abe seethed as I silently reflected on the fact we had gone back to using formal names. "Abe and I are currently en route to Phoenix. You are to stay put—that means in your house, with Nicoh nearby—until we arrive. We can discuss future logistics at that time, but under no circumstances are you to go anywhere, alone or otherwise, until we knock on your front door."

Perhaps I'd had too many Wheaties this morning. Usually, I knew better than to open my pie-hole while the tiger was pacing. "But—" I started.

"Shut it!" Abe growled, immediately cutting me off, though the angry temperature of his voice had reduced significantly since the aforementioned butt-chewing.

I'd never had older brothers, but I was guessing this was what it must be like. What a treat. My deepest sympathies go out to all the little sisters in the world.

"So, are we all on the same page?" Elijah asked once his brother had finished, though he wasn't really asking. "You will remain where you are until you see our beady little eyes staring back through your peephole. Is that clear?"

I mumbled a curt "yes," hoping when they arrived six hours later, I would finally be allowed to come out of the corner and take my dunce hat off.

CHAPTER TWENTY-NINE

After my illuminating call with the Stanton brothers, I powered my cell phone off. I needed time to think. Good thing I had at least six hours on my hands.

Did I take Abe and Elijah seriously? You betcha. Don't get me wrong, despite their good looks, those boys could be pretty darn intimidating. They did have some valid points—I hadn't been particularly careful the past few days—and besides, it wasn't going to kill me to cool my jets for a while.

I settled on the couch and proceeded to sift through the photos Daniels had supplied while Nicoh placed his large head on my feet. I opted to look through the Alcore photos first, which included many of the same people as the one he had shown us earlier, in similar poses. Perhaps it had been an attempt at a public relations photo-op?

I had hoped for a more detailed shot of Alison Anders, but the angle and distance were consistent from one photo to the next. Still, I was drawn to her face. It was like looking at a time-warped version of myself. Although her mouth was serious, her eyes were warm, the same shade of blue, with a hint of violet. Her soft reddish-brown hair, though styled more simply than was typical for the era—it was the 1980s, after all—cascaded over her shoulder in a long ponytail. No-nonsense bangs framed her heart-shaped face. I shuddered, the resemblance was downright eerie.

My thoughts drifted to the woman I'd known to be my mother, who had raised and nurtured me, given me unconditional love. While there had been several similarities—it was the woman in the photo who had given me life.

I lingered on that for a moment. Had Alison survived, would she have loved me as equally? My eyes drifted to her left hand. It was pressed, almost protectively, against the base of her ribcage, right above her tummy, exposing the small swell I'd missed before. Even with her roomy lab coat, it was obvious she was pregnant. I looked again into her eyes and found my answer.

I shuffled through the rest of the photos, wishing Daniels had provided a date and some names to identify the members of the Alcore team. My wish was partially granted when I flipped to the last photo in the stack. Someone had neatly typed the name of each person in order of appearance and row on a sticker affixed to the back of the photo. I glanced through them and not surprisingly, only recognized Alison's name. There was still no date, but Alison and her baby bump made the timeframe a bit more definitive.

I moved to the GenTech photos, which differed from Alcore's in that they were of smaller groups of three to four people, all at work in what appeared to be various locations of the lab. Working on the Gemini project, perhaps? This time, each photo was labeled with a date and the names of the people in the image. I panned through several, searching the names, looking for one in particular.

I was about halfway through the pile when I found it—a photo of Martin Singer. The photographer had captured three-quarters of his face. He was ruggedly-handsome, with dark eyes and sharp, angular features that would have made him look severe, had it not been for the mop of wavy brown hair that brushed the base of his neck, giving him a boyish, playful look.

Based on his facial expression, he was deep in conversation with the man to his right, who was looking—no, glaring—directly into the camera, as if annoyed by its presence.

Taking in the man's features, I gasped—not because his stare seemed to bore through me—because he looked eerily similar to someone else I had seen recently, also in a photograph. My heart clenched as I checked the name on the back of the photo. I double-checked. The label identified the man as Theodore Winslow. Coincidence? Definitely not.

There was no doubt in my mind Theodore Winslow was Winslow Clark's/Tanner Dolby's father.

My mind started racing. Daniels had said only mothers had been cloned, resulting in female offspring. Had he been misinformed? Or lying? Was it possible GenTech had progressed further on the Gemini project than originally thought?

I wondered who had taken the photos. There was no signature or copyright on the back. Convenient. Could it have been Daniels' mysterious Mr. X? There were so many pieces to the puzzle strewn about, yet I had a sneaking suspicion we were closer than we thought. I pulled out a stack of index cards and started writing the items we had learned to this point.

It had started with Alcore and GenTech. Both had initiated controversial human cloning projects, funded by the same sources. GenTech had reportedly progressed more quickly, producing several successful offspring while Alcore had struggled, yielding none. GenTech was quick to conceal their results—possibly to retain their competitive advantage over Alcore—by severing the connection between the mother and children shortly after birth, using the pretense of a secure adoption.

Enter the Sterling Joy Agency—owned by GenTech—managed and operated by the conveniently missing Maxwell and

Mavis Baumgardner. Sterling Joy appeared to exist for the sole purpose of unloading Gemini's offspring. By separating the twins, then adopting them to parents in different states, they were able to assist GenTech in concealing the project's secrets.

In doing so, the Baumgardners retained Jonathan Silverton as their lawyer to oversee both sides of the adoption and serve as liaison for the agency. Silverton seemed to work exclusively for Sterling Joy, as no other clients were ever identified. That being the case, he was likely at the forefront of the interactions between GenTech and Sterling Joy and could easily have been singled out as the scapegoat if and when crap hit the fan.

I wondered if Silverton had gone to his grave feeling remorse for his involvement, essentially off-loading cloned babies for GenTech, spreading them throughout the country to childless, unknowing couples. Had he been alive, I would have asked him.

If he had felt remorse, had he forwarded the birth certificates and other documents on to the Winestones? I tended to think he had. I also believed he had sent the same documents to my parents, the ones that had upset my dad shortly before he and my mother perished in the plane crash.

Had those last repentant acts also made him a liability? If so, had his stroke been induced—made to look like an accident—as a means of averting a repeat performance? I realized I had identified far more questions than answers, all of which would need to be given some more thought. In the meantime, I returned my attention to GenTech.

GenTech employed Martin Singer, one of five scientists, on the Gemini project. Martin had an affair with Alison Anders, a researcher for the competition, on a similar, less successful cloning project. Although Daniels said X never spoke of their involvement or even indicated anyone had ever been the wiser, someone at GenTech had known enough to pay for Alison's medical bills after her death. Paid, despite the fact Martin had allegedly removed the formulas and destroyed the Alcore lab once the project had been terminated. Yeah, right.

If that weren't crazy enough, there were the events surrounding our births. Before Alison went into premature labor, she and Martin happened to make arrangements with the Sterling Joy Agency in the event they both unexpectedly died? Arrangements—as in separate adoptions—which also happened to be the status quo for GenTech at the time. Conveniently, both Alison and Martin passed within days of one another, and the adoptions went off without a hitch. I shook my head. Something didn't sit right with me. A lot of things, if truth be told.

There was also the recent discovery of Theodore Winslow, who—after seeing the father-son similarities—was likely Clark's/ Dolby's father. Winslow, also a scientist, worked side-by-side with Martin at GenTech. What was the state of their relationship? I wondered. Not to be cliché, but they say a picture is worth a thousand words, and if the pictures I had seen were any indication, it was tumultuous at best.

Had Winslow used the project to produce his own clones? Had Martin felt the need to remove the formulas and procedures from GenTech because of people like Winslow? Finally, had Winslow sought revenge against Martin by turning his son into a manipulator and cold-blooded killer?

I was contemplating the validity of that theory when the doorbell rang, forcing Nicoh into his grumbly guard dog mode. I looked at my watch. Abe and Elijah had made good time. I rose, squinted through the peephole and after taking in their stern looks, mentally prepared myself for a continuation of the morning's butt-chewing as I opened the door.

"Why is your cell phone off?" Abe growled before I had an opportunity to speak. Though Nicoh was familiar with Abe and his brother, he was wary of the tone and quickly moved his body protectively between us.

I scruffed Nicoh ears gently, ignoring the question. "Well. Hello. To. You. Too. You two made good time. Won't you please come in?" My voice remained calm. Pleasant.

Elijah huffed out something that sounded like "hi" and pushed passed his brother, apparently taking me up on my offer. Nicoh and I moved to the side as he entered. Abe scowled but muttered his own greeting and followed.

"I turned my cell phone off so I could think. After the reaming you two gave me earlier, I took some time—" I had prepared a little mea culpa speech, but Abe put his hand up to stop me, his expression softening, and when he spoke, it was not the incensed tone I had anticipated. It was one of concern.

"We're sorry, AJ. We were worried when we couldn't get a hold of you. After everything that has happened…" he looked down at his feet, unable to finish his thought. A moment passed before Elijah completed it for him, his voice uncharacteristically shaky.

"What my brother is trying to say is we care about you. We don't want you getting hurt on our watch." Abe looked up for only a moment to affirm what his brother has said, then sullenly resumed staring downward.

Understanding washed over me. They were unable to contact Victoria that last day. In their race to reach me, they feared history had repeated itself.

"Ohhh, I'm so sorry. I didn't think." I choked back a sob, awkwardly balling my fists at my side. Now I was the one left staring at my shoes.

Abe shocked me when he pulled me into a tight hug, a motion which almost forced tears to spring freely from my already dampened eyes. He released me and Elijah followed suit, enclosing me in a massive bear hug. At this point, all three of us sported red-rimmed, dewy eyes, which thankfully, none of us was quick to point out.

Once we had all recovered from our moment, Elijah was the first to speak, "AJ, we've got some news. Anna called us while we were on the road. She heard from Paul Switzer at the Jaguar dealership over in Malibu." He let out a deep breath before proceeding, "Tanner Dolby is dead. His body was found in a ravine near Big Bear by a couple of hikers. The condition of the body was pretty degraded, but the medical examiner's office was able to make an identification based on dental records. Anyway, they estimate he'd been dead at least eight months."

"Before the Winestone's accident," I said quietly, positive the colored had drained from my face.

He nodded. "And before the falsified mix-up with Mrs. Winestone's Jag."

"How did he die?" I asked.

"Undetermined. Could have been anything from exposure to a fall. There wasn't enough left."

I shook my head. "It doesn't matter. I'm pretty sure he left this world with help from his twin brother, Winslow Clark."

CHAPTER THIRTY

I showed Abe and Elijah the photos Daniels had supplied, including the one of Martin Singer and Theodore Winslow, then shared the conclusions I had drawn, adding in the one I had formulated about Tanner Dolby and Winslow Clark being twins, rather than the same person. It was the only way he could have been in two places at the same time. One was dead in a ravine while the other worked at the Jaguar dealership in Malibu. Actually, if you added in his stint as a crash site investigator, that would make it three. Regardless, the former Clark/Dolby, now Clark, had been a very busy, very bad boy.

When I finished, Abe excused himself, stepping outside. "Let me give Anna a quick update. She's still trying to track down a co-worker of either Martin's or Alison's and this information could be useful."

"Pretty sketchy, huh?" I asked Elijah.

"I wouldn't say that," he replied, "though it would be helpful to know more about Martin's working relationship with Winslow."

"I could give Daniels a call, see if X had mentioned anything specifically?" I shrugged.

"Worth a shot," Elijah agreed.

Several messages awaited me as I powered my cell phone on. "How many times did you two call me, anyway?"

Elijah grinned at me sheepishly. "Uh, maybe a couple?"

I laughed while I dialed the number Daniels had supplied during our visit. The older gentleman picked up on the first ring, and once greetings were exchanged, I asked him about the GenTech scientists. Abe came in the front door and tucked his cell into his pocket as I hung up with Daniels.

"Everything cool?" I asked.

He gave me a quick thumbs-up, indicating Anna was good to go.

"So, I called Daniels while you were outside and asked him if X had ever mentioned the working relationships among the scientists at GenTech, and he literally burst out laughing. He asked if I meant the ongoing feud between Theodore Winslow and Martin Singer."

"Interesting," Abe commented as Elijah nodded.

"Their relationship was contentious, at best. X told Daniels the two were often seen in heated arguments and while it didn't turn physical, it caused a great deal of tension for the entire Gemini team."

"Any idea what fueled it?" Elijah asked as he settled on the couch, Nicoh nestled comfortably at his feet.

"Egos?" Abe offered.

"Indirectly, yeah. Martin felt Winslow was pushing the project farther and farther into moral and ethical gray areas. You know, the kind that makes you feel squishy just thinking about them?"

Both Abe and Elijah both shook their heads in the affirmative. Abe made himself at home on the other end of the couch, opposite his brother, while I paced.

"Martin tried to rein Winslow in and even attempted to get the other team members involved, but Winslow was the lead scientist, which gave him a great deal of authority and control over the project. Most were afraid he'd boot them off the project or make it difficult to move to another if they challenged him, so he was basically allowed to do as he pleased."

"Jerk-wad," Abe grunted.

"Major jerk-wad," I corrected. "Regardless, Martin remained diligent in his efforts to keep Winslow under control and remained a thorn in his side until the project was dismantled."

"Martin wasn't afraid Winslow would oust him?" Elijah asked.

I shook my head. "Winslow may have been the lead but Martin had a sharper mind. He needed Martin. Unfortunately, from what X told Daniels, he used Martin as well, taking Martin's formulas and tweaking them to fit his own purposes, which tended toward the—"

"Squishy gray areas?" Abe finished my sentence.

"The squishy gray areas," I agreed. "Anyway, I'm guessing Winslow was pretty bent when Martin snatched the formulas and project procedures."

"Bent enough for revenge," Elijah stated, more than asked.

We all looked at one another. It was definite possibility. But after thirty years?

I remembered I hadn't listened to my messages and quickly dialed my voicemail as I went to the kitchen for beverages. There were eleven waiting for me. Eleven? I glanced back at the two and smiled.

Both were working hard to be Nicoh's favorite. Abe was giving him belly-scratches while Elijah mussed his face and ears. Delighted whoo-whoos filled the air as Nicoh reveled in the extra attention.

The first three messages were from Abe and Elijah, clearly not happy campers. The fourth was from Leah, about four hours earlier, letting me know she would be working late on a story and would catch a ride home with her editor. Her editor? Ok, that was weird. I continued to listen to rest of the messages. All were from Abe or Elijah. The content, more of the same. I shook my head. They were persistent, I'd give them that. I was about to send a snarky comment to that effect in their direction when my phone rang.

By the time I finished the call, I had dropped the phone on the floor and collapsed to my knees. My body shook as Abe and Elijah rushed to my side.

"It was Leah's editor," I whispered, barely able to form the words. "He wanted to know when he could expect to see her today. He said he knew we were working on a side project and if she didn't want to jeopardize her current job, she needed to check in ASAP."

I took a deep breath and upon noting their confused expressions, added, "I dropped Leah off in front of her office building over six hours ago. One of the messages was from her, a couple of hours later, telling me she was working late and wouldn't need me to pick her up after all," I choked out the last words, a sob threatening to break free. "She said she was getting a ride with her editor. *That* editor."

Abe and Elijah moved to the floor with me, a brother flanking each side.

"AJ—" Elijah started, rubbing my arm tenderly.

I didn't give him a chance to finish, "He has her, doesn't he? Clark has her."

I looked at them both earnestly, but regardless of the response, I knew it was true. Leah told me as much in her message. She wouldn't ask her editor for a favor, much less catch a ride with him. Ever. Period. She knew I'd known that and used it as a means to let me know something was awry.

"We need to call Detective Ramirez," I said firmly, without waiting for a response.

"Agreed. I'll handle it." Abe patted my hand as he rose from his squatted position and moved into the kitchen, already dialing.

"He'll need an update," Elijah called after his brother.

An update, meaning from the time Ramirez called to confirm the identification of Tanner Dolby's car to the discovery of his body in Big Bear. It was a call I was glad I wasn't making. Best to let them talk ex-cop to cop. Regardless, I had a feeling Abe would be earning his keep on that one.

Elijah looked at me for a long moment, and I realized he was still holding my arm, almost as though his grasp was keeping me upright. Perhaps it was. Finally, he spoke, his tone quiet, but even. Confident.

"We'll get her back AJ, I promise."

Before I had a chance to respond, my cell phone rang. Fortunately, it still worked after I had dropped in on the hardwood floor.

"It's Leah's number!" I exclaimed, tilting the screen so Elijah could see.

He nodded. "Put it on speakerphone."

I did, and at his second nod, answered it, "Leah?" I heard a mechanical click on the other end.

"Arianna? It's me. I don't have much time."

It was a recording. Though her voice echoed over the speakerphone, she sounded so small, so alone. My heart clenched for my best friend.

"He wants to make a trade. You…for me. My office building…the thirty-first floor in one hour. The key card for the elevator is in your mailbox. Don't bring the cops. And don't be late."

The recording ended and so did the call. I couldn't do anything but stare at the phone lying in my outstretched palm.

"She must be so scared," I uttered, barely a whisper, my heart breaking into a million pieces.

Had he hurt her? Or worse? I hadn't heard Abe come back in. He gently took the phone from my hand, and for the second time that afternoon, pulled me into a hug.

"It'll be ok, AJ. She'll be ok. I promise." Both brothers had given me their word in as many minutes.

As I pulled away, I looked each of them in the eye. "I'm going to hold you to that. Both of you." Pulling myself together for Leah's sake, I asked, "Now, how are we going to do this?"

Twenty minutes later, we had formulated a plan and were en route to Leah's office building. Ok, it wasn't much of a plan because Clark held all the cards, but it was something. I was glad to have it, as well as Abe and Elijah on my side.

I knew Clark had purposely selected the thirty-first floor because the top ten floors in Leah's office building were currently empty. Number thirty-one was smack-dab in the middle of the empty floors, meaning there would be no traffic coming or going and no neighbors above or below.

I hated to think how he had managed to secure a key card or when he had slipped it into my mailbox. The mere thought of him being that close to me—ugh. I needed to stop that type of thinking and focus on the plan.

Abe and Elijah would accompany Nicoh and me as far as Clark would allow. Leah had specified no cops and perhaps we had taken liberties with that statement, but for the time being, that didn't rule out everyone else. I'd much rather have them cooling their jets on the elevator than thirty-plus floors out of reach.

Ramirez would have an undercover team waiting at a safe distance, but since we'd decided not to risk wearing any special gadgets Clark might find, they'd be flying blind, waiting only on signals from Abe or Elijah. Yeah, like I said, not much of a plan. It wasn't something I could control, or worry about. I'd let the rest of them do that. For now, all I could think about was Leah.

I was surprisingly calm as the four of us entered Leah's office building, my mind clear. Even Nicoh stood at attention, his head held high, despite being tethered to my side. Abe and Elijah were equally stoic, clad in all black ensembles, one flanking us on each side. From the hostile, almost frightening expressions each wore, I was glad they were on my team.

Clark had selected a time of day where the hustle and bustle of the workday had long subsided and we moved easily through the lobby to the bank of elevators that would take us to the thirty-first floor. As the massive doors slid shut, I caught a glimpse of a figure lingering next to the faux palm trees that lined the hallway. Our eyes connected as the gap disappeared and the elevator began its ascent.

Ramirez.

It lasted seconds, but the ride to the thirty-first floor felt like an eternity.

"You sure you're ready to do this?" Abe asked, his tone was one I would have expected him to reserve for a comrade heading into battle, not for a hysterical photographer with knocking knees and sweaty palms.

I gave him a curt nod. Sure, why not? I thought to myself. I was ready. I did this kind of thing every day, between picking up dog doo and dealing with self-important, entitled clients like Charlie. Oh yeah, here it was, on my daily to-do list: rescue best friend from maniacal killer. Easy peasy. Rah. Go, team. I blew out a deep breath as the elevator slid to a halt, then inserted the key card Clark had supplied. The doors screeched opened, resembling fingernails on a chalkboard. Fitting—in a Freddy Kruger sort of way.

We peered around as we edged out of the elevator and found nothing but a hallway leading to the left. A sharp voice boomed over the intercom, nearly piercing my eardrums, "Ms. Jackson. I need you to throw that key card as far down the hallway as possible. No girly throws, please." I tossed the card as requested and it landed about fifty feet ahead of where we stood.

"Very good, Ms. Jackson. I guess lugging all that camera equipment around does a body good." Obnoxious. "Your arm candy can step back into the elevator. Their job is done here. They may return to the lobby and tell Detective Ramirez to get his men out of the building while making sure they do the same. In the meantime, I need you and your canine to move slowly down the hall."

Great. I glanced one last time at Abe and Elijah and gave them a single head nod. Their faces were stony and expressions unreadable as they moved onto the elevator and the doors closed. I waited until I heard it descend before advancing slowly down the hall.

I reached the end before I heard the voice again. This time, it was almost conversational, the frosty tone gone, "Ah, finally, we are alone. Please turn right. You will see a series of concrete posts immediately to your left. Select one and secure the canine's lead to it. I'll wait." How considerate, I thought snarkily as I turned into an expansive, unfinished room.

The floor hadn't been built-out yet, so all the beams, wiring and fluorescent lighting remained exposed. I saw the concrete posts the voice had referenced and made a show of looping Nicoh's lead around it twice before tying it off.

His warm eyes bore into mine, pleading as I took his big head in my hands and whispered, "I love you, Nic, be a good boy while I get Leah."

He started to howl when I moved away, so I stretched out a hand, touching it gently to his nose.

"It's ok, baby." He tilted his head, obviously not satisfied, but ceased nonetheless.

"Oh my, what a well-behaved pet. One can certainly appreciate that." The voice laughed, sarcastically." Jerk-wad. "You'll be happy to know your bodyguards complied—handsome couple, by the way—and your cop friend and his donut-eating buddies have officially left the building."

More laughter. Grating. No one likes a comedian who laughs at his own jokes.

"It's a lovely evening, Ms. Jackson. Please join us on the veranda."

Veranda? Give me a break. I moved through the open space, thankful the lights were on as I made my way to the opposite side of the floor, where I assumed the patio was located.

As promised, Winslow Clark waited for me in the broad entrance that led to the outdoor patio, looking like he had walked straight off the pages of *GQ*. His sun-bleached hair was slicked back off his tanned face, exposing his piercing blue eyes and too-too polished teeth, visible through his fabricated smile. He was dressed to the hilt in what looked to be an Armani suit of exceptional cut, a crisp white button-down dress shirt underneath. Shoes were of the Italian variety, with a high gloss sheen I could have probably seen my reflection in.

"You like the suit?" He preened, waving his hand in a downward motion. "I borrowed it from my brother when he graciously lent me his identity. Guy had great taste, but his choice of professions? Commission-only? In this economy? You've got to be kidding. Besides, who wants to stand around talking about a Jaguar all day? Totally overrated. All the fun is in driving it." More boisterous, annoying laughter.

I ignored Clark's attempt at banter. "Where. Is. Leah?"

"Oh come on, Arianna. You're no fun. Leah said you'd be fun. Now I'm not so sure."

I seriously doubted Leah had said anything of the sort. He stepped backward onto the patio and nudged something with his foot. There was a built-in planter in the way so I couldn't determine what *it* was, though I had a bad feeling.

"Hmm. Looks like Leah's not going to be any fun for a bit, either."

Gasping, I stepped forward slightly—just out of Clark's reach—so I could get a better look. I could almost make out Leah's crumpled form at the base of the planter. She wasn't moving.

"What did you do to her? Is she…is she…"

"Relax, Arianna. Take a load off. She's fine. I gave her a little something to help her…mellow out," he said, laughing at his own little joke. Irritating. "Girl was giving me a raging headache with all that talking. How do you deal with it?"

"I manage fine," I replied dryly. "Are you sure she's ok?"

"Arianna, I'm hurt." He pretended to pout, pulling his lips into a tight frown. "I said she was fine, and she is. She'll be back in the Land of Chatty Cathy in a while."

More laughter. I gritted my teeth. Even under normal circumstances—those being the ones where he wasn't planning on killing me—this guy would get on my nerves. Give him a big fuzzy microphone and you'd have the epitome of a cheesy 1970s game show host. Seriously. It was all I could do not to punch him in the throat. A sudden burst of adrenaline made me decide I would do so later, given the opportunity. For now, I had to keep him talking. So far, so good.

Clark blathered on, "Moreover, we had a deal. A trade is a trade. And it wouldn't be fair if I reneged on my part before we even started, now would it?"

Ah, now we were getting somewhere. "If that is the case, surely you won't mind if I move Leah to the elevator and send her on her merry way? Now that I'm here, that is."

"I would mind, actually. We're getting to know one another and here you are, already making up new rules. Arianna, have I mistakenly given you the impression I would be open to negotiating?" his tone steeled, ever-so-slightly, but enough to let me know I had hit a nerve.

I put on the best remorseful expression I could muster. "My apologies, I didn't mean to imply—"

"Ah, Arianna, I see we are going to get along just fine," he chuckled, "but you simply must call me Clark. Like Clark Kent. I'm dashing, like Superman, aren't I?" My gag reflexes engaged two-fold.

"Is Clark you're given name?" I asked sincerely, ignoring his question. It was likely rhetorical, anyhow.

"It is indeed. Given to me by my father, Theodore Winslow, to whom you've recently become acquainted." At my surprised look —I was truly—he threw his head back and laughed. "Don't be so surprised. I know about all the mischief you and the lovely Leah have been stirring up the past few weeks. Just between you and me, liked her hair better the other way. This screams retro-Meg Ryan. *So* not a good look on her.

"But I digress. Before you ask, yes, my father raised me, if you could call it that. He was truly brilliant, but a bit of a one-trick pony," he babbled. "GenTech, specifically, the Gemini project, was his life. Thanks to *your* father, Martin Singer, my father's work was nearly destroyed."

He leaned against the wall, reminiscing. Obviously, he'd heard the story from his father many times over the years.

"Is your father still alive?" I asked quietly, prompting him to continue, to keep him talking.

"He is, but the loss of Gemini consumed him. Ate at him. Reduced him to nothing but a shell of the man he once was. Even exacting revenge failed to fill the void he felt. That he still feels."

"Revenge?" I was pretty sure I knew what he was referencing, but wanted him...needed him to spell it out.

"Come on, Arianna," Clark shook his head, "I thought you were smarter than this, that you and your chum here had at least the basics figured out." He rolled his eyes at my apologetic shrug but continued, "He killed Alison Anders, of course. To get back at Martin."

I had been prepared for this admission, but mentally shuddered at his cool, nonchalant delivery. I needed to keep my emotions in check for the duration. I was sure there would be more revelations to come. For the time being, however, Clark was engrossed in his tale and oblivious to my discomfort.

"The duplicity of their affair enraged him. Not that he cared they had one, but that they thought they could get away with it. Martin judged and chastised my father for years, calling him immoral and self-righteous. And yet, in the end, Martin was no better. He manipulated the project for his own personal gain while accusing my father of doing the same. My father simply couldn't take it any longer, he had to do something. He developed a plan that would take cunning and patience. However, to reap the rewards, he could wait.

"Once he learned Alison was pregnant, he kept tabs on them, educating himself on their every habit and routine. Alison's premature contractions were his doing—he was a doctor, after all —so slipping the right concoction into her herbal tea while she lunched with friends was easy work for him. It just took a bit of creativity.

"After she went into labor and had given birth to you and your sister, he made a quick trip to the hospital to administer a healthy dose of happy juice to the new mother. Before anyone knew what had happened, it was bye, bye, Alison." Clark sounded so proud, so enamored of his father, I wanted to vomit. I palmed my fists at my sides. Keep it together, I thought to myself.

"Despite having pulled one over on Martin—who was devastated by Alison's death—his revenge was short-lived. GenTech lost its funding and pulled the plug on Gemini. It wouldn't have been so bad, had Martin not subsequently destroyed or taken everything pertaining to the project. Once again, my father had to act. And quickly. He even coerced the Baumgardners and their lawyer, Silverton, into fabricating the adoption paperwork he would later slip into the hospital files. All that remained was taking care of Martin."

"He killed Martin, too?" I asked, my tone casting doubt. Tread carefully, I told myself.

Unaffected, he nodded. "Only after he had given Martin every opportunity to come clean, to tell him where the formulas were. Martin refused, of course, so father had to help him see the error of his ways. I'm sure Martin had plenty of time to contemplate that during his trip off the Skyway Bridge. No pun intended." He smirked and though I hadn't flinched, added, "Oops. Too soon? Sorry, my bad." Internally, I barely managed to contain myself, though my face remained a blank slate.

Nonplussed, Clark continued, "Anyway, with Martin out of the picture, the Baumgardners stepped in to stake their claim, as was their legal and dutiful right, and presto, little Victoria and Arianna got new lives." He threw his hands up, as if announcing we'd won a prize, not lost our birth parents.

I ignored him. "So why'd he go to all the trouble of fabricating the documentation? Why take the risk? Why not kill us?"

"All great questions, Arianna. I'm so glad your brain has decided to join us. From the look on your face the past several minutes, I wasn't sure you possessed one." What a jerk. "It was mostly curiosity and convenience, at first. And as it turns out, the best decision he ever made."

"What happened to the Baumgardners?" I asked.

"Dead. That witness, Sophie Allen, too," he responded lightly, as though I had asked him whether he took cream or sugar in his coffee. "Father planted a few false stories to make it seem as though they had abandoned the adoption business to pursue other opportunities, things of that nature."

"So, their deaths…were your father's doing?" Clark nodded,

before adding, "Of course, once I was old enough, I helped him out when I could. You know, first with the lawyer, Silverton. Old fool was on borrowed time, anyway. A bad heart and all. I helped ease him into the next life once he started getting sentimental about the old days, sending copies of stuff he shouldn't have to your parents and the Winestones. Of course, I had to clean up that mess, too."

I took a deep breath, readying myself for whatever Clark was about to dish out. I knew it would be bad. Keep him talking a little longer, I thought. Just a little longer…

"Do you realize how hard it is to make a plane crash look accidental?" He grinned, clearly enjoying himself, then continued without waiting for a response. "I had no idea. I won't go into all the gory details, but once it was done? What a rush. Love your pop's D-backs hat, by the way. It's one of my all-time favs," he paused to wink while I tempered my emotions, my heart thudding heavily against my chest.

"Though it wasn't as fun, it did make the Winestone's car accident that much easier, less of an impact and all that, but you take what you can get. Tanner, of course, was the easiest to deal with."

By this point, my fingernails had cut into my palms, making them bleed but still, I had to keep it together. I looked at Leah's prone body for strength and proceeded.

"You…killed your own brother?"

"Yup, gave him a bit of a helping hand while he was out hiking near Big Bear. Boy, was he surprised to see me. It was almost as though he had seen a ghost." He laughed raucously, as I thought back to what Bonnie had told Abe, Elijah and Anna about Victoria the day she had taken the photo from the dealership.

"Anyway, we were brothers by blood only. It's not like we grew up together or anything. He went the Sterling Joy route." As if that explained everything away.

"I never met Tanner-boy until the day he met his maker. Guy was a tool, a real waste of space. My father would have been insulted to know that had come out of his gene pool. It was my duty to handle it before Father could find out."

"What about Frederick Glass, the guy who took ownership of Mrs. Winestone's Jag?"

"At your service," he chortled. "Clever, huh? And just for the record, the Winestone's car was sweeeet. I was actually sorry I had to leave it sitting in that to-remain-unnamed location. Let's just say I'm sure the locals took good care of that fine piece of machinery."

I glanced at Leah again, who still appeared to be unconscious. I prayed that he had only drugged her and that after all of this, she'd be ok. With that in mind, I proceeded with the question I had wanted to ask Clark from the beginning.

"Why Victoria? Why did you kill my sister? Was she getting too close?"

His reaction was not at all what I had expected. "Too close?" He burst out laughing. Loudly. Harshly. Gloating. "Don't you get it? You and Victoria *were* the key all along. Martin gave you both a gift. And thanks to you, *my father's* work—Gemini—will rise again."

Whatever he had anticipated my reaction might be after that announcement, it was not a blank stare. He threw his hands up, thoroughly exasperated.

"You still don't get it, do you?"

I shrugged. "What gift?"

He huffed, still piqued by my underwhelmed response.

"It was two actually. Two gifts. The first is your very existence. Proof of Gemini. Proof of its success." He slapped his hand against his leg after each sentence for emphasis.

"Proof of my father's success," I carefully corrected, purposely stepping into dangerous territory, "but no matter, the question remains, if it was such a gift, then why kill Victoria? Why threaten to kill me?"

Either oblivious to or choosing to ignore the slight I had made to his father, he snickered. "Because of the second gift, of course. In those early years, my father was so blinded by rage he over-looked the bigger picture.

"Martin may have taken the formulas, but he would never have destroyed them. He would have kept them safe. In a place that was logical. Logical to a scientist. He would have kept them with the daughters who were born out of his work." He bobbed his head with excitement.

"My father realized Martin had made only one visit to the hospital after Alison died. During that visit, he injected each of you with a chip that contained one-half of the formulas. That way, someone—that someone being me—would have to get to each of you in order to get the whole enchilada." He grinned as he dug into his pocket. "In fact, here's the one I beat out of Victoria." He held up something that looked to be no bigger than a rubber pencil eraser, tossed it into the air and caught it easily before putting it back into his right trouser pocket.

I thought about Victoria's face the night I had found her in my dumpster, and though I was completely shocked and repulsed by his revelation, it was time to turn the tables on this little production before he did the same to me.

"It took your father thirty years to figure *that* out?" I threw my head back and laughed heartily, throwing in an obnoxious snort for good measure.

As I had anticipated, the temperature of the room shifted. Clark's eyes went cold. Wild. His smile morphed into a contemptuous sneer. Suddenly, several things seemed to happen all at once. Clark pulled a vicious-looking knife from his waistband and lunged in my direction. I charged at Clark's weak side, arms up protectively, ready to defend. What can I say, never bring a girl to a knife fight.

Nicoh charged around the corner and barreled into Clark's midsection, knocking both him and the knife to the ground. Leah scrambled from her prone position, a rock from the planter in hand, and conked the sweet spot on Clark's melon.

While I was pretty sure Nicoh had successfully knocked Clark out with his maneuver, this was a situation where it was definitely better to be safe than sorry, so we found an extension cord and hog-tied him to one of the concrete posts.

Leah might have also kicked him a couple of extra times to make sure he was out. He was. Sweaty and exhausted, both mentally and physically, we sat on the floor and hugged Nicoh, who panted with delight.

Neither of us spoke for a long moment until Leah broke the silence, "I'm not sure where Nicoh learned those moves, but it certainly wasn't from the Brazilian Butt Lift workout videos you've been watching."

We both laughed shakily, just as the cavalry burst in. Ramirez and his guys led the pack, followed closely by Abe and Elijah. Worried expressions quickly turned to surprise as they surveyed the scene. Don't quote me, but I was pretty sure I heard a "bad ass" from one of Ramirez's team members.

True to form, Leah and I looked at one another before turning to the lot of them. "What took you so long?" we both asked, drawing chuckles from the team.

Only Ramirez failed to crack a smile. Instead, he stepped forward until the toes of his boots were touching mine—I was wearing Chuck Taylor's, but you get the picture—and he was looking squarely into my eyes.

"What took you so long?" he grumbled after a long moment.

I gave Leah a sideways glance, and she did the same.

Ramirez's stern expression broke as he erupted into laughter. The whole room followed suit.

"You saw that?" I chirped as quietly as I could. More laughter filled the room as Ramirez nodded.

"And heard it, too. We had guys on the roof of that building." He pointed to the adjacent office building. "Guys on the roof of this building. Mics in the ceiling of the floor below—"

"I get it. I get it. You saw. You heard," I interjected.

"And we acted," Leah clarified.

"Risky maneuver," Ramirez countered.

"But effective." She was still pumped up and ready to take on anyone who dared give her guff.

Ironically, Clark chose that moment to regain consciousness. Before he had a chance to struggle, however, Leah marched over and kicked him solidly in the gut.

"I happen to like my hair, you ass."

CHAPTER THIRTY-ONE

A couple of days later, Ramirez, Abe, Elijah, Leah, Nicoh and I were sitting at Starbucks. Would you have expected us to be somewhere else? Even Anna had driven over from L.A. and after meeting her in person, both Leah and I proclaimed her as our new BFF. The guys gave us the requisite eye rolls in response. All was good in the world.

After hog-tying Clark, the FBI had swooped in, taken over and whisked him away to parts unknown. Ramirez muttered something about jurisdiction, but I had a feeling it was a lot more than that.

Clark's father, Theodore, had been located in Virginia Beach and taken into custody, though the FBI hadn't been particularly forthcoming about what would become of either of them. One thing was for sure, both would have a lot of 'splaining to do. I hoped, at a minimum, they'd be cooling their jets for a long, long time, in a very secure location.

All of us had gone rounds with the FBI, for all the good it did. They were still skeptical about the Gemini project, as well as the whole GenTech/Sterling Joy angle, though my gut tells me they knew more than they let on.

In the meantime, I filled both Cheryl Earley and Sir Harry in, as promised. Abe, Elijah and Anna also let Switzer know what had happened to Tanner Dolby. He hadn't hired a bad guy after all. Dolby just had the misfortune of being in the wrong place at the wrong time. Well, that and being born into a bad gene pool. Anyway, they never did find Mrs. Winestone's car.

As for the children of the Gemini project—where they ended up was anyone's guess. Without the benefit of the Baumgardner's documentation, it could take months, if not years, to track them all down. Besides, there were other ramifications associated with springing that jack-in-the-box.

I still didn't have answers to all of my own questions, either. For now, I was completely content sipping an icy latte with friends and, of course, celebrating Nicoh's new hero status. He had, after all, saved our bacon and was currently reaping the rewards, as scratches were plentiful and scones were in full supply. A favor, though? Let's keep that bacon comment to ourselves. I wouldn't want him assuming he could break into full-howl mode every time he wanted a few dozen pieces—cooked extra crispy—added to his nightly food bowl. I was cringing at the thought when Leah's voice brought me back to the present.

"So, are you really a clone? It would certainly explain a lot," she teased.

I nodded. "It isn't conclusive yet, but it's looking like Martin and Alison combined their knowledge and resources for the benefit of their own side project, for a lack of better words. The tests I had run yesterday will positively confirm one way or the other. I need to sit tight and wait for a few weeks until the results come back."

"If they come back positive, does that mean Martin wasn't your real father, after all?" Elijah asked. "Rather, he was the father of the invention, so to speak?"

"Not necessarily. While the Gemini project isolated cells

solely from the mother, X recently told Daniels that Martin and Alison had developed a way to introduce a few of the father's cells during the chemical alteration phase. If this was indeed the case, the resulting offspring would still retain all the physical characteristics of the mother but could also take on other characteristics of the father."

"So the children would still physically look exactly like the mother, but could take on say…the father's knack for science or math?" Abe asked.

"Yeah, something like that," I laughed.

"Is that how Theodore Winslow created Tanner Dolby and Winslow Clark?" Anna questioned.

"X said Winslow morphed many of Martin's formulas to create his own special hybrid offspring. He basically wanted to replicate himself," I replied seriously. "All he needed was a surrogate."

"Wow, what an ego." Abe shook his head. "But what happened to the surrogate?"

"I doubt we will ever know," I replied.

"You think we can trust X's word?" Elijah asked. "And who is he or she, anyway?"

It was Leah who responded, "We don't know for sure but so far, X has been right on the mark."

Everyone groaned.

* * *

Several caffeinated beverages and much reminiscing later…

Ramirez needed to leave to start his shift, so I offered to walk him to his car. He had been noticeably quiet all afternoon, despite the fact I had apologized repeatedly for my previous bad behavior. I wondered if he would ever forgive me and was about to ask him as much when he surprised me by bending over and placing a gentle kiss on my cheek. I stuttered, struggling to find the appropriate words and when I finally mustered the nerve to look up, found him chuckling softly.

"Looks like I finally figured out a way to get the last word in, Ajax."

He winked as he got into his cruiser and drove off. After a moment, the left-hand side of my mouth quirked into a small smile.

"Game on, Detective. Game on."

* * *

Everyone at the table had watched in amused silence as the scene between AJ and Ramirez played out.

While AJ stood in the parking lot, watching Ramirez drive away, Anna leaned over to Abe and Elijah, raised her finger to her lips and whispered, "I think Ramirez has a crush on AJ."

At their flabbergasted expressions, she and Leah turned to one another and pretended to clink their Starbucks cups in a mock toast before bursting into uncontrollable giggles. AJ joined them, and soon the entire table bubbled with laughter.

All was good in the world, indeed.

EPILOGUE

Leah went to my appointment with me. Even though I was only having a standard MRI procedure done, I was still scared to death and needed my best friend there to hold my hand. She did so as long as she was permitted and even then, talked the technician into letting her stay in the observation room for the duration. Despite having to stay in one place longer than I had at any other time in my life, I made it through with flying colors.

The radiologist confirmed I had a chip, no bigger than a pencil eraser, embedded in the soft tissue directly behind my left ear. Though I strongly suspect she mistook it for an electronic identification marker, she made no comment, and I offered nothing in return. I had received the answer I had gone there looking for.

Leah continued to baby me as we left the office, insisting I stay put while she got the car from the parking garage and pulled around to get me. After seeing her use her powers of persuasion on the technician, I quickly conceded, electing to sit on a small concrete bench in front of the medical complex.

While I waited, I slipped the chip from my pocket and let it sit in the center of my palm. Victoria died trying to keep me safe, because of it. If and when I had its partner removed, decisions would need to be made. I closed my hand. For now, I would keep it—keep them—safe.

When I glanced up, a figure stood directly across the street, facing me. Smiling. From a distance, the features looked vaguely familiar and once I squinted, giving them detail, there was a hint of recognition.

Leah pulled to the curb, distracting me. I smiled warmly at my friend, and as I approached the car, a burst of wind blew loose strands of hair into my face. In the moment it took to brush them away, the figure was gone, leaving nothing but an imprint on my mind. I joined Leah in the car, and soon after I rested my head against the seat, found myself dozing.

During my slumber, the figure reappeared. Still smiling, he stepped across the street until he stood directly before me. As we faced one another, he extended his hand, palm upward so that I might grasp it with my own.

"Hello, Arianna. It's nice to finally meet you," he said as I took his hand, his smile broadening.

"Hello, Martin."

~ The End ~

ABOUT HARLEY

Harley Christensen lives in Phoenix, Arizona with her significant other and their mischievous motley crew of rescue dogs (aka the "kids").

When not at her laptop, Christensen is an avid hockey fan and lover of all things margarita. It's also rumored she's never met a green chile or jalapeño she didn't like, regardless of whether it liked her back.

For more information on the author and her books, please visit her at www.mischievousmalamute.com.

OTHER BOOKS BY HARLEY

Mischievous Malamute Mystery Series
Book 1 ~ Gemini Rising
Book 2 ~ Beyond Revenge
Book 3 ~ Blood of Gemini
Book 4 ~ Deadly Current
Book 5 ~ COMING SOON!

Six Seasons Suspense Series
Book 1 ~ First Fall
Book 2 ~ Winter Storm

23410922R00098

Made in the USA
San Bernardino, CA
24 January 2019